"A moving, humane tale of life lived in history's long shadow."
—*Booklist* **(starred review)**

"Platzová's prose is as sharp and effective as the angles of an expressionist monument. . . . [A] powerfully elegiac novel."
—*Publishers Weekly*

"A Czech novel about art, death and sex set against the backdrop of the Holocaust and never-ending war. . . . The reader comes to connect with and care for [Platzová's] characters as more than mouthpieces for history." —*Kirkus Reviews*

"*Aaron's Leap* takes you on an epic journey, which is also a very intimate and personal story—entertaining, touching and brutally honest. Her characters are full of compassion and tenderness, but are never sentimental. It's a great book."
—**Agnieszka Holland**, Academy Award-nominated writer and director of *Europa Europa* and guest director of HBO's *The Wire* and Netflix's *House of Cards*

"This young author's book immediately caught my interest for its narrative mastery and remarkably skillful identification with the complex atmosphere of the interbellum era. . . . [A] brilliant novel."
—**Ivan Klíma**, Franz Kafka Prize-winning author of *Waiting for the Dark, Waiting for the Light* and *My Crazy Century*

"Told in clear and beautiful prose, *Aaron's Leap* is a deeply moving portrait of love, sacrifice, and the transformative power of art in a time of brutal uncertainty."
—**Simon Van Booy**, author of *The Illusion of Separateness*

The
Attempt

The
Attempt

Magdaléna Platzová

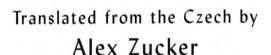

Translated from the Czech by
Alex Zucker

BELLEVUE LITERARY PRESS
NEW YORK

First Published in the United States in 2016 by

Bellevue Literary Press, New York

For Information Contact:

Bellevue Literary Press
NYU School of Medicine
550 First Avenue, OBV A612
New York, NY 10016

Originally published in Czech as *Anarchista* © 2013 Torst and Madaléna Platzová.

Library of Congress Cataloging-in-Publication Data
is available from the publisher upon request.

Bellevue Literary Press would like to thank all its generous
donors—individuals and foundations—for their support.

This publication is made possible by grants from:

 MINISTRY OF CULTURE CZECH REPUBLIC This translation was made possible
by a grant from the Ministry of
Culture of the Czech Republic.

 The New York State Council on the Arts with the
support of Governor Andrew Cuomo and the
NYSCA New York State Legislature

 **National Endowment for the Arts** arts.gov This project is supported in part
by an award from the National
Endowment for the Arts.

Book design and composition by Mulberry Tree Press, Inc.

Manufactured in the United States of America.

first edition

1 3 5 7 9 8 6 4 2

paperback ISBN 978-1-942658-08-5

ebook ISBN 978-1-942658-09-2

For Jiří

To be a man, a complete MAN.

— Alexander Berkman

The
Attempt

PROLOGUE

BY THE TIME I GOT TO THE CAMP, it was already dark. I went straight from the airport. It was a cool October night, drizzly, with a wind blowing in from the west. The wind was stronger toward the southern tip of the island, swirling through the old tenements with their strings of tiny lighted windows.

I had a backpack, a warm coat, and a sleeping bag.

I breathed in the damp smell of underground and fog that always lets me know I'm in Manhattan.

I stopped at the outer edge of the encampment, on the border where it ended and the police zone began: service vehicles with flashing lights, vans, extension ladders. Dozens of raincoated cops.

The camp was set in the ground below street level. I walked down the stairs. At first, all I could see were dark sheets of plastic, billowing and snapping in the wind like sails.

Once my eyes adjusted to the lack of light, I was able to make out the people squeezed in at the eastern end, where the stairs formed a kind of amphitheater. They stood calmly and quietly, letting the water run over them. Nobody had an umbrella. A girl was explaining the voting rules. Her voice kept getting lost in the gusts of wind, but the ones closest to her repeated her words loudly after each sentence, so even the people all the way in the back could hear.

I walked down the main path, which ran from east to west through the improvised shelters. I passed the kitchen, where homeless people lined up for food; an information table and a station distributing warm clothes; a tent with a sign on it proudly proclaiming LIBRARY. At the lower end of the square, I found myself alone. Across the street, cranes jutted skyward around the floodlit skeleton of the unfinished new World Trade Center. I found the tree, encircled by a ring of granite benches.

I picked up two sheets of the cardboard that was lying around everywhere. I put my backpack down on one and sat down on the other. The rain was letting up. I spotted a few stars in the cracks between the scudding clouds.

I pulled out my phone and texted: "I'm here. Waiting at tree. Jan"

A moment later, an answer beeped back: "Five min. Marius"

— I —

American
Footsteps

I

'D ALWAYS WANTED TO LIVE IN NEW YORK. Right in Manhattan, in one of those high-ceilinged gloomy apartments lined with bookshelves that were ingrained in my memory during the short trip I took there as a teenager and which I've associated with intellectual life ever since. Dark apartments with a view into the windows of the apartments across the way, where the ghosts of old Europe lounged about beneath yellow lamp shades and in purplish clumps of dust. Where the damp smell of the subconscious wafted up from the drainpipes and ventilation shafts.

I couldn't tell you the origin of my desires. The images I identify with, where did they come from? Family legends? Books? Childhood memories? In times of crisis, our secret longings emerge, hurling us forward, drawing us in like a planet sucking up a handful of cosmic dust.

Around the time of my thirty-fifth birthday, I felt like a horse harnessed to a cotton gin. I always made a point of taking the tram in to work, to make the trip last as long as possible, and one day on the tram I decided to write down a list in my notebook of all the things I would never do. Just to give myself some perspective, get it all down in black and white.

1. I will never write a novel.
2. I will never make love with another woman again.

3. I will never move from one friend to another, with nothing except a backpack of books and a toothbrush.
4. I will never learn proper French.
5. I will never live in New York City.

That was just four years ago. I smile when I think back on it now. You've got to keep hope alive. That and faith in others, who, like my ex-wife, have plans of their own.

One day my wife decided to find someone else to provide for her, and suddenly I was a free man. I applied for a scholarship to a university in New York. Gave up my job at the paper. Cut down my workload at school to part-time. Moved in with friends. Decided to take up history again. And write. But before any of that, I made love with a woman who wasn't my wife. I crossed that off my list first.

There's actually a theory I have connected to my image of New York. It goes back to 1925, when my great-grandmother Friederike married a man from a town in northern Bohemia. With one edge, one corner of my heart, it also relates to my best friend, Josef, who planted two fixed ideas in my head: one, that writing is the best vocation in the world, and, two, that I'm not actually the great-grandson of the factory owner Emanuel Schwarzer, as I've always assumed, but the great-grandson of the Russian-American Jew and anarchist Andrei B., with whom, in 1924, my great-grandmother Friederike had an affair in Berlin.

I WAS BORN IN PRAGUE in the early seventies. By that point, my family's upper-middle-class origins were ancient history. My grandfather, being half German, had his property confiscated by the Czechoslovak government after World War II. They told him he should be glad they hadn't run him out of the country. The only thing they let my family keep was a caretaker's apartment in the north Bohemian town of L., in a villa we got back—one of the few things returned to us—after the revolution in 1989.

The house had been built before World War I, with glassed verandas and Art Nouveau friezes on the walls, and a half-timbered gable that my great-grandfather had had decorated in the mid-twenties with a sign in elegant script reading VILA FRIEDERIKE. Till the day she died, my grandmother Týna tended to the garden, which no longer belonged to her. For as long as she could grip the pruning shears, she trimmed the rhododendron and azalea bushes and poked around the rock garden, her pride and joy. The space tucked away under the old yew trees, with the red trunks of the pines tilting precariously over them, seemed mysterious to me as a little boy. Every summer I built my bunkers in a different place, together with Josef, who lived with his proletarian parents on one of the upper floors of our villa. He was four years older than I was and had already read a great deal.

Nothing changed when the villa was returned to us. My parents were still young and had too many ambitions of their own to pour money into the upkeep of a ramshackle house. But they weren't ready to sell it yet, either. I visited L. to see my grandmother, until she died, and later on to see Josef. In 1999, the year I got married, Josef published his first book. His parents passed away and his sister got married, so he was left on his own. He moved out of the beautiful third-floor apartment into the caretaker's apartment my grandmother had been living in. By day he worked in the local secondhand bookstore and by night he wrote, slowly blossoming into a true eccentric. When he published his second book, I used my contacts in Prague to help him get a review in one of the papers. It had no impact either on sales or on Josef's fame.

The last few years before he died, Josef was obsessed with Andrei B., a Russian anarchist who, he claimed, was my real great-grandfather.

Over and over, he read and reread the few letters from Andrei that Friederike had neglected to destroy, searching for clues and hints. Written in English, they clearly highlighted the one area where, despite their strong sexual attraction, there was friction: Friederike merely flirted with the idea of equality. Flirting was her life philosophy. She was also much younger than Andrei, who at the time had been in his fifties.

Josef was fascinated by anarchism but still couldn't quite fathom it. He had read Bakunin and Kropotkin in the original, studied the legacies of Nestor Makhno and Emma Goldman.

It can't just be dismissed, he maintained. Even Sartre in his twilight years declared himself an anarchist. It was the only label he was still willing to claim.

Speaking of labels: Among the stacks of unfinished projects, in one of the boxes Josef had confided to my care, which his sister helped me load into the car immediately after his funeral (she wanted to be rid of his things as soon as possible), I found a notebook labeled ANARCHIST. It was an unfinished text, apparently notes for a novel that Josef had planned to write at some point. Inscribed in green ballpoint on the cover of the blue notebook filled with finely ruled graph paper, it said: *Compassion as a chest wound. There is no way of life that accords with our conscience. The anxiety. Everything was easier under totalitarianism. Freedom opened up an abyss too deep for me to see its bottom.*

2

SUMMER, NEW YORK, RAIN. At the ticket counter of the Kolman Museum, I purchase an overpriced ticket from one of the ladies you see volunteering at every New York museum. With their surgically smoothed faces and wrinkled, gold-laden hands, they look like antiques themselves.

The lobby is dark, a set of French doors giving on to a garden where the rain drizzles into a marble pool overgrown with water lilies. The wooden floor creaks beneath the luxurious carpet; the showcases along the walls are filled with porcelain. A cord blocks the staircase leading to the upper floors. Everything above the first landing is drowned in darkness. Green velvet drapes cover the windows inside the rooms. When I draw them back, I can see Central Park.

I've been in New York two weeks now and still can't believe it. I feel like an actor on a movie set. Central Park, the Metropolitan Opera House, Fifth Avenue. Last Wednesday, at the suggestion of one of the other students from my university, I took the ferry that shuttles back and forth between lower Manhattan and Staten Island. It's free and as good as any sightseeing tour you can take. I didn't expect to be so moved seeing the smoky blue of the Statue of Liberty.

ONE GORGEOUS VERMEER, two El Grecos, some Renaissance Italians, and *The Education of the Virgin* by Georges de La Tour. The rest is mostly kitsch: idyllic landscapes, a fluffy Fragonard, portraits of languid ladies by Burne-Jones and Whistler. An odor of dust issues from the tapestries and shelves of antique books. The whole opulent mansion feels like a prison, a den where some old rodent comes to deposit its prey.

Kolman's daughter Eleanor, who after her father's death had the building converted into a museum, is painted next to her father in a dual portrait that hangs above the fireplace in what used to be the study. His manly profile stands out sharply in the foreground: a white-bearded chin jutting forth dynamically, a straight, short nose, a low-hanging brow, and a small round head of meticulously groomed white hair. Half-hidden behind him, as in a fog, is the face of a young red-haired woman, wrapped in a light muslin veil of the sort ladies used to wear to shield themselves from the sun.

The museum also has a cinema screening a film titled *J. C. Kolman: Collector and Philanthropist* every thirty minutes. There's only fleeting mention of the assassination attempt; nobody is named. On the other hand, there's plenty of footage of a sparkling pond with ducks paddling across the surface—to evoke a feeling of serenity, I assume. The credits list Eleanor C. Kolman as chief consultant on the project. Her mother, Alice, appears only once, in a wedding photo from 1882. After that, not a single mention. Where did she go? What happened to her? Why isn't there a single trace of her in the house where she lived for thirty years?

I come home from the museum and sit by the window a long time, looking out at the street. It has stopped raining and the air is thick with humidity. I watch as a man in a bright-colored shirt, with carefully smoothed gray hair and a strong nose that reminds me of Josef, pulls the remains of a sandwich from a trash can, removes the foil wrapping, and lays it out tidily on a concrete pedestal. He crosses himself and eats standing up, a look of deep satisfaction on his face.

THE WOMAN IN THE REFERENCE LIBRARY of the Kolman Collection suddenly got her guard up when she realized what I was looking for.

"How did you know we have that here?"

"It says so online."

"Where exactly?"

"In your catalog."

"Are you sure it isn't Eleanor Kolman's correspondence you're looking for? We have that here, of course. Everything that relates to the collection."

"No, these were the letters of her mother, Alice."

She picked up the phone and dialed the archive.

I explained my request again to a young woman who introduced herself as Julie.

"We have some of it here," she admitted. "What do you need it for, though?"

"I'm a historian from Prague and I came here on a research scholarship. I'm doing a study of American women at the turn of the twentieth century. Did you know the wife of the first president of Czechoslovakia was American? Have you ever heard the name Masaryk?"

She handed me a form to fill out: name, address, telephone

number. Plus a statement saying I wouldn't quote from any material without the express consent of the Kolman Reference Library.

"Which period are you interested in, exactly?" asked Julie.

"I'm interested in all of it."

She appeared with a box a few moments later. She asked me to place the letters back in their envelopes when I was through with them, and said with a smile as she walked away, "Alice had terrible handwriting. Totally illegible, you'll see."

The box contained a series of folders labeled by year, beginning in 1882, the year of Alice's wedding. The last letters had been painstakingly transcribed by someone on a typewriter; the others, as Julie had warned me, were nearly impossible to decipher. From John C. there were only a few decorative courtship cards: "My dear Miss Alice, it would be an honor if you would accompany me to the horse races tomorrow afternoon. . . ." Then just some telegrams sent from a steamer crossing the ocean from the New World to the Old. A few postcards from Europe.

There was almost nothing from the period around 1890, except a clipping from the *Chicago Herald* about the Johnstown flood.

I love the feel of old letters, and when the librarian wasn't looking, I quickly stole a sniff.

Eagle Rock, Massachusetts, 6/4/31

Dear Ellie,

Since you want me to write you regularly but complain that you cannot read my handwriting, I have decided to dictate my letters.

I am dictating this to Miss Bodley, who was kind enough to bring her typewriter into my bedroom so I can lie down while I "write." The one disadvantage of this arrangement is that I won't be able to complain about Miss Bodley. Not that I have reason to.

There is not much news. As soon as I arrived, I asked to be shown around all the rooms (or at least I think all of them; I am not even certain how many there are). I found everything entirely in order, apart from a wet spot on the ballroom ceiling, and the railing on the grand terrace will need to be repaired and a few cracked tiles will need to be replaced.

If you could see the wisteria! It is splendid this year. It hangs like a canopy over the entrance, climbing up to the windows on the second floor.

The peonies and irises are also in bloom. The roses haven't frozen.

The rabbits had babies. Just these silky little balls. I held them in my hands awhile. Maybe we could sell them—twelve dollars a pair? Think about it.

That's all for now. Soon Simon will be calling me down for lunch.

Write soon, and above all, do come.

Your loving Alice

Eagle Rock, Massachusetts, 6/10/31

Dear Ellie,

The weather has been steady, sunny but not too hot, practically made for going on walks and horseback riding. Your room is ready; you can come anytime.

The wisteria is slowly losing its blossoms, as are the peonies, but the jasmine and some of the roses are starting to bloom. This morning in the garden, Simon cut me the most beautiful bouquet you can imagine, but I had to have it taken away, as the smell gave me a headache.

If you can imagine, Mr. and Mrs. Smith are on their honeymoon. They are constantly all over each other, Mr. Smith ruffling Mrs. Smith's feathers. I had the cage moved closer to my bed so I could see them better.

Have you given any thought to those rabbits?

And are you coming soon? I didn't understand what you said on the phone. What are you waiting for?

I send you kisses and look forward to seeing you.

Your mother

Eagle Rock, Massachusetts, 6/12/31

Dear Ellie,

Today I have great news. Imagine, if you will, Mrs. Smith has laid an egg. There's only one and Mr. Smith is sitting on it. It seems the honeymoon is over. Mrs. Smith just sulks about and sharpens her claws in the corner. They don't say a word to each other. I just hope the egg stays warm; it would be nice to see the little one peck its way out.

There's nothing new otherwise, except perhaps that Miss Bodley and Miss Lindsay took the car into the city by themselves and landed in the ditch when they swerved to avoid a horse and buggy. Nothing happened to them, and they both laugh when they tell the story. Now Miss Bodley is frowning, saying that she doesn't want to write about it, but what other news have I got? Miss Bodley is a darling, and for that matter so is Miss Lindsay, who is such great fun. She has begun to learn ancient Greek and is planning a big trip to Europe along with Miss Bodley.

Yesterday Simon brought me the first strawberries; they were delicious. Soon we will have cherries and apricots, too. I shall send you a basketful if you don't come before then. But I would really much rather you came.

The peaches on the south side of the house should also ripen this year, provided there is enough sun. The weather is steady, warm but not hot, much more agreeable than in New York.

I send you kisses and remain ever yours,

Mother

Dear Ellie,

Only briefly today, the weather is muggy and I am not well; even dictation exhausts me. I had them carry me out to the terrace, but it wasn't agreeable and I felt even more tired afterward. I'm better off inside, here in the bedroom.

There is no news. Perhaps only that Mr. Smith had a quarrel with Mrs. Smith and pushed the egg out of the cage.

Lately I have no appetite, which is making Simon sad. He spends all day preparing delicious food for me and I barely even touch it. Have you thought about when you will come? And for how long? Only because you asked about it on the telephone, I will say I still suffer from constipation constantly. The doctor says it's due to my long-term use of laudanum.

Kisses, Alice

Eagle Rock, 7/15/31

My dear Ellie,

You needn't worry about me. I am sure I will feel better once the hot spell has passed. This morning we had a great commotion. The caretaker's dogs raided the henhouse and throttled several hens and a number of chickens. They didn't even eat them, they just did it for sport. Naturally, they were punished for it.

The Mapplethornes are marrying off their second daughter; the ceremony will be next Sunday at their home on Long Island. Could you order a set of dishes and send them as a gift in my name? 145 or 150 dollars should be plenty, no more than that.

Also, I forgot to tell you on the telephone that I've ordered a new carriage. The contract says they have to deliver it by no later than the thirtieth; otherwise I won't pay.

It should be here by the time you arrive.

Kisses, your mother, Alice

7/27/31

Dear Miss Kolman,

I tried to reach you by telephone, but I had no luck, and in any case the news I have to share with you is better written than said over the phone.

Your mother has, unfortunately, not been well these last days. It may be because of the heat wave we've been having. Madame Alice practically doesn't go out, remaining indoors all day with the blinds pulled down. She refuses to eat. Occasionally, we manage to talk her into a bit of broth or a glass of milk, but she refuses solid food.

Dr. Hartley, who comes to the house every day, considers your mother's condition to be quite serious and advised me to tell you not to postpone your visit for too long.

Apart from that, however, your mother remains balanced and takes delight in the smallest details: a flower or a plate of fruit. Even if she does not eat the fruit, she likes the smell and enjoys touching it, especially the peaches. She says they remind her of her children's faces. I have the impression Madame Alice no longer recalls some of the events of her life.

Dr. Hartley is of the opinion that unless Madame Alice's condition improves significantly and she begins to eat again, the situation won't last any longer than a week.

Your room is ready; we'll be expecting you.

Respectfully,

Nancy Bodley

Julie was standing behind my back. "We'll be closing soon. I can leave the box here for next time, if you want. Will you be ordering any photocopies?"

3

SATURDAY MORNING, MY PHONE RINGS. The display shows a local number, here in New York. Who could it be? Apart from a few administrators at the university and the head of my department, I don't know anyone here yet. I haven't gotten in touch yet with Professor Kurzweil, whose book-cluttered apartment made such an impression on me twenty years ago. I had come to New York for a week from Washington, D.C. It was late February. When I walked out of the station building onto the street, it was dark and snowing heavily. I can still see it as if it were yesterday: the wind driving the wet snow down a long corridor of buildings as escaping steam rises from the pipes underground.

My phone is still ringing.

"Hello?"

"Mr. Schwarzer?"

"Yes."

"Jan?"

"That's me. How can I help you?"

"This is the office of John C. Kolman the Third, I'm sorry to bother you. Were you at the reference library of the Kolman Museum yesterday? Did you give this number as your contact?"

"Yes."

"I'm very sorry, Mr. Schwarzer, but I'm calling to tell you

the library staff made a terrible mistake. They shouldn't even have let you in."

"Excuse me?"

"There is a regulation," says the woman on the other end. "Please don't take it personally, but there is a regulation prohibiting anyone German from entering the library. Originally, it also applied to the collection. That was changed. However, there's nothing that can be done when it comes to the library. I'm afraid I must inform you that yesterday was your last visit."

"But I'm not from Germany."

"You have a German name."

"Half the people in the Czech Republic have a German name."

"Were your parents German?"

"No."

"Can you prove it?"

"I have a passport. And a birth certificate." I can't help but laugh.

"You have a birth certificate?"

"I'm sorry," I say, "but I don't think I understand. . . ."

"If you don't mind," the woman says slowly, sounding out her words, "could you bring your documents in to Mr. Kolman's office? Eight one three Madison Avenue. It's on the corner of Madison and Sixty-eighth."

"When should I come?"

"Right now, if you want. We're here. Be sure not to forget your birth certificate. Oh, and one more thing," says the woman. "Our staff photocopied some letters for you yesterday. Could you bring those with you as well? In the event the matter fails to be resolved to your satisfaction, we'll have to ask you to return them. Of course there's no way for us to verify it, but I hope you will respect our rules and refrain from making another copy."

"But I paid for them."

"Naturally, we will reimburse you. It isn't your fault. Thank you again for your cooperation, and see you soon."

THE STUDIO APARTMENT I RENT from the university is on the West Side of Manhattan, near campus. I can catch a bus cross-town to the East Side and walk the rest of the way. I'm sure I'll find a shop somewhere on Lexington to make a copy of Alice's letters.

Along the way, I wonder how it is they maintain such distinct boundaries between neighborhoods. Even just a few blocks away, the sharp-dressed men of Madison Avenue are nowhere to be found. They cling to their territory like lizards.

A Korean manicurist sits inside a beauty salon, staring out the window into the street. Her face is white as wax, round and perfectly symmetrical, motionless as the bright yellow orchid blossoms keeping her company in the window.

On the corner of Madison and Sixty-eighth, I find the building the woman described to me over the phone. The lobby has thick carpeting, crystal chandeliers, velvet sofas, and a polished gold-plated table with a big bouquet of white irises on it. One of the men at the reception desk calls upstairs, then walks me to the elevator and rides with me up to the fourth floor, where he lets me out in the entryway of a residence.

Margaret is a young woman with very blond straight hair, dressed in a red suit and white silk blouse.

"Will you still be needing access to the library?"

"Yes, that's why I came."

I pull out my birth certificate. The court interpreter in Prague wrapped his English translation in a tricolor ribbon and affixed a stamp of the Bohemian lion. What more evidence could she want?

She reads it through carefully, then shakes her head, running a polished nail down the names of my parents and grandparents. "Schwarzer, Jäger, Goetz. These are all German names."

"As I told you, half the people in my country have German names."

"How is that?"

"Migration. Austria-Hungary . . ."

"I see."

"So where did this strange rule come from?" I laugh. "Discrimination on the basis of names?"

"Discrimination, yes, quite right." Margaret nods. "But there's nothing we can do about it. Mrs. Eleanor C. Kolman was the one who introduced the rule, and made several other things conditional on it. Legally, our hands are tied. Mr. Kolman can explain it to you himself."

"Mr. Kolman?"

"Yes, he'd like to meet you. He likes to meet everyone who's interested in his family. I'm sure once you explain what it is you're interested in, it will be fine."

"What do you mean?"

"He'll let you into the library, honey." Margaret bares her teeth at me. Her lips are painted red and she has a thick layer of makeup, but no mascara or eye shadow. Maybe she's allergic to them.

"Just a moment, I'll announce you," she says, picking up the phone. When she puts it back down, she says, "Mr. Kolman says to go ahead in."

I need to use the bathroom, but Margaret has already opened the door.

GREEN CURTAINS. THE WINDOWS in the study of John C. Kolman III are covered in heavy green velvet curtains, just as in his great-grandfather's house. A lamp shines on his desk. The walls are paneled floor to ceiling in dark wood and are hung with paintings: a view of the Hudson, a still life, and a portrait of a man wearing a black suit and sporting a neatly trimmed white beard.

Along with his great-grandfather's name, the young Kolman inherited his wide, low brow, strong jaw, and bright blue eyes. He also has a smaller frame, with broad shoulders and a short neck. Apart from that, he looks the same as half the other men in the neighborhood. Bright dress shirt, open at the neck, with a light sport coat and close-cropped blond hair. He's suntanned and bristling with energy, as if he just jumped off his yacht.

"What can I offer you? Water, coffee, whiskey?" He shakes my hand. Two white rows of teeth shine dazzlingly. "Have a seat."

I plop down into a leather chair. Sure, I'll have a whiskey, why not?

"It's a pleasure to meet you," he says.

"Likewise."

"Ice?"

"Yes, thanks."

"I'm interested in anyone who's interested in us."

I smile, but lacking the training of my American counterparts, the muscles in my face cramp up.

"Naturally, I'm always eager to know what it is, exactly, they're interested in. We've had bad experiences, too. With so-called historians. You understand. One can never be too careful."

I gather up my nerve. "Why the regulation about the German names?"

Kolman sighs. "There's really nothing we can do about it. I can't tell you how much embarrassment it's caused us. We've had to turn away some famous art historians, professors from German universities. Even though it's been years since the war. But I'm afraid Aunt Ellie won't budge, and she inserted the rule so cleverly into the foundation's bylaws, it's impossible to get rid of it. She just doesn't like Germans, period." He laughs. "Just like President Wilson."

"So you mean she—Eleanor C. Kolman—is still alive?"

He nods his head. "Incredible, isn't it? Of course the rule has its reasons," he goes on. "Ellie was a brave woman. In 1918 she went to a field hospital on the western front. She saw the slaughterhouse in France, but mostly she saw bombed-out cities, churches in ruins. She never forgave the Germans for that. She has a photo album, you know. Filled with pictures of shattered cities next to postcards showing the way the cities looked before the war. Whenever someone in the family objected to the ban, she would show them the photos and say, 'The monsters who did this don't deserve to come anywhere near a work of art ever again. The rest of the world might not care, but I do. I will not let them see our paintings.' Then came World War Two, and that only strengthened her in her conviction. The first thing she did was have a bunker built, where the entire collection could be moved. She was obsessed with the idea that the Germans would bomb New York. The Allied bombing, oddly enough, didn't upset her. Medieval towns in Germany leveled to the ground, Tokyo firebombed . . . But that's Aunt Ellie. She sees only what she wants to see. It wasn't until ten years ago that the foundation's board of trustees got her to rescind the rule, at least for the museum. It was pretty embarrassing having to throw tourists out. When it comes to the library, though, I'm afraid she has sole jurisdiction."

"But I'm not German. I'm Czech."

"Whose side did your country fight on in the Great War?"

"You mean World War One? Austria's." I blush. "But there were Czechs who fought on the other side. In France. Russia. England. And after the war, we got our independence. Did you know the state of Czechoslovakia was officially born in Pittsburgh?"

"No, I did not." John C. sighs. "But tell me, what makes you so interested in my family that you requested the private correspondence of my great-grandmother?"

"I'm doing a study of the daughters and wives of American entrepreneurs from the turn of the century."

"But what made you choose the women from *my* family?"

"They won't be the only ones, of course," I say. "I'm also looking at women from the Rockefellers, the Morgans, the Guggenheims. . . ."

"I see."

"It's a fascinating topic."

"I'm sure. You say you're here on a scholarship?"

"Yes."

"I don't have too many connections to academia, but my father taught at medical school. And my grandfather was a university professor. I was always more the business type, like the old man." He gestures, grinning, to the portrait. "So the scholarship you got was for this project?"

"Not exactly."

"Then what for, may I ask?"

"I also study East European history."

"So what does East European history have to do with the women of the Morgan and Rockefeller families, or, for that matter, my great-grandmother?"

The answer, of course, is nothing. But it does have something to do with the Polish, Czech, and Slovak immigrants who worked till they spat blood in the factories owned by Kolman's great-grandfather. And with Russian anarchists.

"It's a personal project of mine."

"I'm through interrogating you." Kolman waves his hand. "My aunt would never allow any exceptions. She's a stickler for principle. The regulations are clear: no German names. And your name sounds very German. I'm sorry about that. Did you bring the letters?"

"Yes. You want them now?"

"Please, if you would. I trust you haven't made other copies?" His smile is meant to suggest the question is just a formality. But his eyes are dead serious.

"No."

"Do forgive us. We've had some very bad experiences. You'll have to make do with the Rockefellers. Here's a tip for you:

Abby Aldrich Rockefeller. She played a major part in bringing European modern art to America. Or the women from the Whitney family. They even set up their own museum." Kolman stands from his chair.

"I'll look into it," I say.

He walks me to the door and gives me a gentle pat on the shoulder.

"I'm glad I could be of some small help."

"Thank you very much."

"Have a nice stay in New York."

Margaret must have been listening on the other side of the door. She returns my documents to me without a word and escorts me into the hall, where the doorman is waiting for me in the elevator. A minute later, I'm out on the street.

I spend the rest of my Saturday angrily Googling John C. Kolman III to try to find some dirt on him, some present-day Homestead or Johnstown. Not a thing. If that slimeball really is up to no good, he's keeping it under wraps. All I find out is that he has a sister. She entered a convent years ago and changed her name. The convent is in Arizona, near Phoenix. I send out a probe in her direction via e-mail.

4

SHE SITS ACROSS FROM ME, SMALL AND DARK. The blond, blue-eyed Kolman men all married black-eyed brunettes. Sister Michaela's eyes are the same shape as those of her great-grandmother Alice, but they aren't weighed down with pain. There's a lively shine to them.

Sister Michaela is happy to be in New York. Scanning the people, sipping her cup of coffee, turning her head in excitement as a fire truck goes wailing by outside the window. She says at home she sees the same thing every day. The mountain at whose base the convent is located shimmers like a mirage when the air is hot and in winter is coated with snow. A group of clouds can often be seen floating motionless at its peak. The surrounding plain is strewn with rocks and overgrown with prickly bushes and cactus plants. Sometimes it's a bloodred, tinted purple; at others, it's a burnt orange or pale yellow. Twice a year, after the rains, it turns green.

The convent is a pilgrimage site. People travel the dusty road from Phoenix and Tucson to visit and stay awhile. The convent puts them up in return for a contribution. They can eat and pray with the nuns, learn to make candles and soap, help out in the garden, tend to the convent's chickens, goats, and donkeys.

Sister Michaela is wearing a dark travel dress. She left her heavy black-and-white habit at home. Instead of a veil, she wears a beret. The last time she was in New York was two years ago, for her father's funeral. She's here again now because she needs money.

"I come from a family of millionaires, but still I have to beg my brother for every dollar," she says. "When I entered the order, my father decided that meant I was mentally unfit, and he wrote me out of his will. At the time, I didn't care. I didn't want anything from my family. But I've changed my mind since then. Not for myself, but those funds can be put to good use. After my father died, my brother contributed to the convent in his name, thinking that would get me off his back, but no such luck. We're building a new church, a refectory. . . . The money goes out as fast as it comes in. The mother superior entrusted me with a special mission."

"Thank you for making time for me," I say. "For being willing to meet."

She smiles. "Seeing as you went to the trouble of finding me . . ."

She is probably in her forties, but as she eagerly drinks in her surroundings, she looks just like a little girl. Only the wrinkles around her eyes give her age away, and her hands, which are slightly red and dried out from working in the dirt, with close-trimmed nails.

I recount my meeting with John C. Kolman III. She shakes her head.

"We must seem crazy to you. It's just that my brother's incredibly touchy when it comes to our family. He feels like he took over the torch of our family honor from Aunt Ellie. He acts as if the whole world doesn't care about anything except history, when the truth is that no one could care less what happened in 1892."

"I do."

"You can read about it in any book. The whole thing was described in detail, ages ago. Whether my family talked to the historians or not. You can't keep the truth quiet for long, not here in America. Whether or not it changes anything is another story."

"I tracked down everything about it I could," I say. "How the unions called a strike at the steel works John C. Kolman ran for Carnegie. How your great-grandfather put down the strike, how many workers were killed and how many were fired. I know that Kolman took out ads on Carnegie's behalf in newspapers in Prague and Warsaw for men to replace the strikers, and that it was the first armed clash between factory owners and employees. It took the unions a long time to bounce back from that."

"There are letters from Carnegie telling him to put down the strike by any means necessary."

"Yes, I know. And when it was all over, Carnegie quietly got rid of your great-grandfather."

"Kolman detested him for that. He refused to reconcile with him, even on his deathbed."

"One thing I never could find, though, which I was hoping might be in the letters I don't have access to anymore, is how your great-grandmother saw the whole disaster. And the rest of your family."

"And besides that?"

"The assassination attempt."

She waves her hand.

"Are there any rumors in your family about the assassination attempt? Or the years afterward?"

"I don't know. I don't think so. It wasn't something we talked about."

"But you all talk about your great-grandfather."

"Sure, constantly. It's like he still controls everyone. It's awful! Especially Aunt Eleanor!"

"What about Alice?"

"Supposedly, she went insane," says Michaela. "My great-aunt always said her mother went insane. That was it."

"Her last letters don't sound like they were written by a madwoman."

"She suffered a shock," says Michaela, bending and twisting a straw in her hands. "In the space of one year, she had two children die and her husband get shot, and on top of that, it was all over the papers that he was a murderer. Even back then, newspapers printed whatever they thought would sell, as opposed to following any particular political line. One week they'd back the unions, the next Carnegie. My great-grandfather was a windfall for them. He didn't have enough money yet that anyone had to fear him. Even later on, when he was more powerful, he always preferred to stay in the background. The only way he wanted to be seen was as an art collector. Have you seen his collection?"

"Yes."

"Do you like it?"

"There are some beautiful works in it."

"I hate it."

"Do you mind if I ask about the past?"

"Why not? Everyone's got a right to ask. Especially when it comes to people like us. Explain and defend, that's all we do, our whole lives. Or deny, like Aunt Ellie. Why do you think I ran away and left it all behind? I don't want to have anything to do with it, understand?"

The expression of an excited child is gone, and sitting across from me is a troubled woman clearly pushing fifty. She stares into her cup.

"First, little Martha died. That was in 1891, after the Johnstown flood. I assume you already know about that. Another interesting chapter. Martha accidentally swallowed a needle, got gangrene, and basically rotted alive. An ordinary X-ray would have saved her life. In the spring of 1892, when the strike broke out in Homestead, Alice was pregnant again. In the summer, she gave birth prematurely to a boy, who lived less than a month. My great-grandfather mourned the loss of Martha his whole life. He never even had a chance to notice his namesake, John C. Kolman. But it must have been a huge blow to Alice. It was a few more years before Aunt Eleanor was born."

"Do you know your great-aunt well?"

"Of course. I grew up with her. She took me to Europe as a child. She was already very old, but she still had a head on her shoulders. She was the one who got me interested in art. She even wanted to—oh, it doesn't matter. I don't want anything to do with them. This is the last time I'm asking my brother for anything. After this, I just don't care anymore. Old wounds. What do you care about all this, anyway?"

"I'm a historian."

"I don't think I can tell you anything else today. Nothing you can't find on your own."

Sister Michaela stands from her seat.

"When do you go back?" I want to say "home," but I'm not sure if you can call a convent that.

"Tomorrow."

"Could I . . . could I write to you sometime? Would you mind?"

"Why not?" Michaela gives a weary smile. "But I can't promise I'll write back right away. We've got a lot of work at the convent right now. You'd be surprised. A lot of people think we just sit around all day, staring up at the sky."

We shake hands good-bye. Her palm is rough and dry.

On the way home, I see a woman walking down the street, pulling a little girl by the hand. They're both staggering, as if in the face of a strong wind. The girl has the face of an old person and a stiff spine; she is swaying from side to side. Despite the summer heat, the mother is wearing a duffel coat, her straw-blond hair falling down over her face. What basement did they crawl out of? I wonder.

People are like stars. The universe is expanding and the stars are moving farther and farther apart from one another, moving faster than the speed of light, until they cross beyond the point of visibility, until the darkness swallows them up.

5

I N THE EARLY NINETIES, when Václav Havel still ruled from the president's seat in Prague Castle and former dissidents went on TV to debate the meaning of truth and freedom, a young American walked into Josef's secondhand bookshop in L.

He was going back home and wanted to get rid of his books before he left. Two suitcases full. He didn't want any money for them. Josef was one of the three people in town he had been able to talk to at the pub during the two lonely years he spent teaching English at the local high school.

One of the books, published by a small university press in the United States, was an anthology of biographies of the most important anarchists. Andrei B. wasn't one of them, but he did play a supporting role in the story of Louise G., an American anarchist of Russian origin.

There were two photos of him. A portrait from 1892, when he attempted to assassinate Kolman, and a snapshot from the mid-thirties: Andrei on the promenade in Nice, wearing a light suit, cane and straw hat in hand, running to catch up with a group of friends, dominated by the short, broad frame of Louise G.

In the portrait he's only nineteen years old. He looks straight ahead, head tipped slightly back, as if shying away from the lens. Bulging Adam's apple, oval-rimmed glasses. Egg-shaped skull, ears that stick out, a thick head of short black hair. Full lips.

I don't look anything like him. When I was little and my parents and I used to go to the Krkonoše Mountains along the border with Germany, everyone spoke German to me, assuming I was one of the blond East Germans who vacationed there. But Josef insisted that hair color didn't matter. He said I had Andrei's nose and mouth.

As evidence he showed me those photographs.

At the libraries here in New York, I found several books containing more details about Andrei B., as well as more photographs.

Toward the end of his life, he looked like Gandhi. In one photo, he sits at a desk shining with stacks of white paper, and he himself is also dressed in white, bald-headed, with wire-rimmed glasses, exuding an aura of . . . How shall I put it? Peace? Gentleness? Something like that.

"AND IF HE REALLY WAS my great-grandfather?"

I'm sitting in Professor Kurzweil's living room. There are a few more books in the library and a few more wrinkles on the professor's face, but apart from that, nothing here has changed in the past twenty years.

"So what?" The professor shrugs. "Biological fatherhood is overrated. If I had to research whether my great-grandfather, grandfather, and father were really my great-grandfather, grandfather, and father, I wouldn't have time left to do anything else, ha ha ha."

Professor Kurzweil put me to shame when I was nineteen,

and it's no different today. Always on the alert, ready to take a dig. He knows everything there is to know about history. His other passion is psychoanalysis.

"So how far have you gotten?"

"I got stuck on the Kolmans."

"The Kolmans? As in John C.?"

"That's right."

I tell him about my research at the library, my meetings with John C. Kolman III and Sister Michaela. He arches an eyebrow, bemused.

"I wouldn't have thought you had it in you. But why are you so interested? Andrei had nothing to do with them."

"What about the assassination?"

"Assassination attempt," he says, correcting me.

"When somebody tries to kill someone, in a way they're connected forever."

"You make it sound romantic." The professor snorts.

"I'd like to understand what motivated Andrei," I say. "Why would a sensitive nineteen-year-old boy, in love, full of plans and grand ideas, decide to sacrifice his life for the sake of someone like Kolman?"

"Kolman was no different from the other entrepreneurs of his time," says the professor. "Neither better nor worse, maybe just a little more discreet. I would look for the answer more in those grand ideas you mentioned. An ideologue can't fully grasp what it means to kill someone. To him it's just pure abstraction, like scratching out a duplicate entry."

A teacher of mine had put me in touch with Professor Kurzweil, a Viennese native who fled to America at the age of fourteen, when Hitler annexed Austria. My teacher was a history professor who was forced to leave the university during the purges after the 1968 Soviet invasion. He got his job back after the revolution in 1989. During the twenty years he was banned from academia, he worked as a stoker in boiler rooms, but continued his research. He even managed to maintain the foreign connections he had established during the political thaw of the mid-sixties. I had great admiration for him, and attended his secret lectures in the mid-eighties—"apartment seminars," as they were known. My parents, who were loyal to the Communist regime, practically had a heart attack.

I remember the first time I called Professor Kurzweil, twenty years ago, from Washington, D.C., to say I was coming to New York the next day and ask if I could spend the night. He wasn't even surprised. That's how it was in those days, after the fall of the Iron Curtain. Open doors, open hearts; naïveté on both sides. It was a beautiful time.

"Keep in touch," says the professor as we exchange goodbyes. "I might have something for you. Do you know the name Malevich?"

"The historian? I've read something of his."

"He was a good friend of mine," says the professor. "He died last year. Left behind a huge collection of material on anarchists. In fact he was the only one who really focused on the topic. I'll find out what happened to his collection."

We stand in the hallway outside his door. I remember it all so well: mirror, red carpet, floor lamp. . . . Suddenly it dawns on me. "Where is your wife? I didn't even say hello."

"Erica? She passed away two years ago," says the professor. "Now I'm learning to be alone."

6

THAT SUMMER MORNING IN 1892, when Andrei boarded the train in New York, it promised to be a beautiful day, nice and hot.

Louise had accompanied him to the station. As she hugged him good-bye, she thought to herself, For the last time!

It was hard for her to imagine.

Of the journey itself, Andrei wrote, "Every detail of that day clearly etched in my mind."

In his wallet he had just one dollar, enough for a night in a cheap hotel. First thing the next day, he would look up his comrades in Pittsburgh, so he could stay with them. How much time would he need to get everything ready? Two days?

He thought about his mother and his eyes welled up with tears. He wanted to remember her alive.

The last time they had argued, it had been about the girl serving their meal. Andrei couldn't stand it when his mother beat the servants.

"She's no worse than you are."

His mother blanched with rage. "Don't you ever talk to me that way."

She reached out and rapped him on the back of the hand with a fork. He grabbed a glass and hurled it at the mirror—one of the elegant Venetian mirrors that decorated the dining room of their country house.

His mother's rapid exit. Then silence. From that day forward until her death, which came all too soon. She turned to the wall and exhaled. He didn't even get a chance to tell her he loved her. He covered her dead hands with kisses.

He fled to America soon after that. Stayed with relatives but didn't linger long. He and his opinions were just a nuisance to them. At sixteen he was kicked out of school for an essay arguing that God didn't exist. What do you do with a boy like that?

He was seventeen when he came to New York. He spent his first few nights on the street, then found friends, comrades. So much had changed in two years! He had moved in with Louise. And now he had a mission. He had been waiting for it. He knew it would come. This act would be his trophy. His guiding star. Something big and real, which couldn't be undone.

"Outside the train windows," Andrei wrote, "the sun is setting. Cows graze in lush meadows. Families with children stand along the tracks, waving at the passing train. The world could be a good place, too. Good for everyone!"

I'M GOING TO PITTSBURGH BY BUS, not by train. We left Friday afternoon from Chinatown in New York. There were no ripening fields outside the window, just the roadside shoulder and the line of cars passing us. Soon it was dark. I booked a night in a hostel, and the next day I would set out in Andrei's footsteps.

IN 1892, A BROWNISH YELLOW CLOUD of smoke, soot, and ash hung over the city from the factory smokestacks belching flames day and night. The workers lived in single-story dwellings slapped on top of one another, each big enough for two rooms, one family per room. Some homes sat off by themselves, tilting sideways in the midst of a block of demolished or burned-out buildings.

Only the main street was paved in Homestead, a steelworking suburb of Pittsburgh set in the bend of the Monongahela River. All the other roads were dirt. In the fall, until the snows and freezing weather came, and then again in the spring, they turned into a sea of mud. The houses, shops, and taverns belonged to the steel mill owners. When the men drank up their wages, they would shop and live on credit, then spend the rest of their lives working to repay their debts. Until their children took their place.

Today a shopping center stands on the site of the former steelworks, of which nothing remains except a row of tall brick smokestacks. On the other side of the river, slowly decaying under the onslaught of rust, are the blast furnace, walkways, and chimneys of the so-called New Mill, which thirty years ago was still in operation. The tracks lead off to nowhere.

From Homestead I head, as Andrei once did, for the millionaires' district in Pittsburgh's East End.

In those days, coaches issued from the gates of expansive villas surrounded by gardens, bearing ladies dressed in white and their children, squeaky-clean and well fed. As Andrei walked down the street, any doubts he might have had disappeared.

From a distance, I contemplate the home where Eleanor can't die. Nearby, she had another center built to hold the art that wouldn't fit into the museum in New York. She turned the surrounding woodlands into a park and donated it to the city. All in her father's name. The house with the round turrets is also slated to become a museum. They're just waiting for her, its last inhabitant, to die. Then the villa and all its inventory will be taken care of by the foundation that Eleanor has granted a large sum of money in her will. Every single object is to be kept: every book, petticoat, toy, and hairpin that fell behind the headboard.

This museum of happy family life will be the last thing she does for her father.

On a bright Sunday morning, the park around the villa is filled with people jogging, parents strolling with children. Yellow leaves settle onto the baby carriage tops; some of the trees are already bare. Acorns drum against the wooden picnic tables. The air smells of nuts, mushrooms, and damp earth.

Following the signs, I easily find the little walled-off cemetery in the woods. The gate is locked, but I can see in through the decorative wrought-iron bars. Beneath a tidy row of thuja sit four tombstones, two large, two small, one topped by a white angel with drooping wings. That must be Martha's. The little one with no decorations probably holds the baby's bones. And the biggest one is Kolman's. Beneath the hulking tombstone is the concrete crypt in which Eleanor had her father laid to rest. Even after his death, she felt a need to protect him from the hatred that he aroused in people. Beside him, covered by a somewhat smaller piece of stone, lies Alice. They had to bury Thomas Kolman elsewhere. After their father's death, when he found out the will provided for most of the estate to go to Eleanor, he parted with the family on bad terms.

I see the sky dully reflected in the windows of the villa. Leading toward the main entrance is a sand-strewn path, carved into the vivid green of a lawn that slopes gently down toward a greenhouse and garden shed. A hundred years ago, Eleanor must have played there, eagerly watching for her father to come home from work. The turn onto the driveway is made from a quiet street lined with villas, each one a copy of a different historical style, from Norman half-timbered houses to Rococo chateaux. The Kolman house is the ugliest one. You can't even tell which style it's trying to mimic. It's been expanded and remodeled so many times, its original appearance has been completely watered down.

I HIT ON THE PLAN OF HOW to get to Kolman's daughter while I was in the reading room of the New York Public Library, looking through a book about the Kolman house that Eleanor herself put together thirty years ago.

I was amazed at how much Kolman's taste changed in the space of just a few years, how perfect his New York collection seemed in comparison with what was on display in the rooms of the first family residence. It encapsulated the difference between a metropolis and a provincial city, between the mentality of cultured art dealers like the Duveen brothers and the outlook of an unsophisticated businessman, who accumulated works of art solely for his own pleasure.

One of the paintings he bought in his first years of collecting still hangs over the fireplace in the Kolman dining room: Pascal-Adolphe-Jean Dagnan-Bouveret's *Christ and the Disciples at Emmaus*. I verified it from sources more up-to-date than Eleanor's catalog, including an article on the Web site of the Art Renewal Society, a bizarre organization based in New

York that advocates for the rehabilitation of nineteenth- and twentieth-century academic painting.

As an emissary of an organization like that, I might find an open door with Eleanor Kolman. I could pretend I was writing a book about the forgotten victims of modern art and trying to track down every existing work by Dagnan-Bouveret.

The furthest John C. Kolman got in his collecting was the Impressionists, and Eleanor was even more conservative, settling in between the fifteenth and eighteenth centuries. She didn't allow any modern art in the collection, even when it meant clashes with the museum's board of trustees. That made two discriminatory rules: no Germans and no modern art.

I RING THE BELL AT THE GRAY STONE GATE. As I wait, the words of Sister Michaela run through my head: "There's one point on which my great-aunt and I fundamentally disagree: I don't believe in art as a way to salvation. The obscene accumulation of wealth can't be redeemed by collecting pretty pictures, not even if you show them for free! In every other respect I'm like her. Are you surprised? My family would be. They think I'm different and that's why I ran away. But in fact it's just the opposite."

"Do you have an appointment?" asks the woman over the phone at the gate when I explain what I want.

"I sent a letter, but I'm not sure if Miss Kolman received it."

There is a pause, then the woman's voice comes back on: "Miss Kolman got your letter."

"That's great. May I trouble her for a moment of her time, then?"

"She was expecting you yesterday."

"That can't be. I definitely wrote Sunday the twenty-second. That's today."

"She can't see you now. She's resting."

"Please, if you don't mind, could you at least ask her?"

Again a moment of silence, then the woman returns.

"Come back tomorrow morning. In the afternoons she's too tired."

"I'm sorry, but I have to go back to New York tonight."

"That's your problem."

"No, I mean yes, I'll come back tomorrow."

"Be here at nine A.M. You can view the painting, but no photographs. You'll have to make do with the ones Miss Kolman had taken for the catalog."

"Yes, of course. Thank you. Please give my regards to Miss Kolman and tell her I'm looking forward to it."

Silence. The staff Eleanor employs aren't too polite. Apparently, she keeps them on a short leash and a little bit hungry all the time, like guard dogs.

BELOW ME GLITTERS THE GOLDEN TRIANGLE at the confluence of the Allegheny and Monongahela rivers, which then continue on together under the name of the Ohio. The lights from the bridges and skyscrapers, yellow, white, and blue, push back against the cold autumn dark. Supposedly, this is one of the most beautiful views in the United States. The air is fresh and crisp. It's hard to imagine there was once so much smoke and dust that even on a bright day the sun didn't peek through. To get up to the vantage point, I took one of the two old-time funiculars that still climb Mount Washington. There used to be seventeen of them. In those days it was the only way to transport people, supplies, construction materials, even horses up the incline. The roads were too narrow. In 1870, when they built the Monongahela Incline, the young John C. Kolman was just getting into the coal business, manufacturing coke and quickly getting rich.

There's no way to miss the mark he left on downtown Pittsburgh. After his split with Carnegie, he proceeded to build at a furious pace, perhaps trying to prove he couldn't be gotten rid of that easily, he couldn't be erased from the city.

He erected a steel-framed skyscraper, higher than the Carnegie Building, as well as a one-thousand-room, twenty-two-story hotel and a huge arcade of shops and galleries in the ornate neo-Gothic style.

All of the buildings are in close proximity to the prison where Andrei B. spent fourteen hellish years, most of it in solitary confinement. For talking back, refusing to go to chapel. For thirteen of his fourteen years, he wasn't allowed any visitors. Once, he tried to escape.

Three anarchists rented a ground-floor apartment in a building just outside the prison walls. While two of them dug a tunnel, the third spent several hours a day playing piano to cover up the noise. After a few months, they actually managed to dig their way inside, but the map they had, drawn for them by a former prisoner, was wrong. Instead of emerging into a tool shed, as they had planned, the tunnel came out smack-dab in the middle of the prison yard. They were found out, and Andrei went back into solitary.

Under U.S. law, he wasn't yet of legal age at the time he

committed his crime, and his attempted murder had failed. The twenty-two years he was sentenced to, later reduced to fourteen, was an unusually severe punishment, even by the standards of the day.

A good lawyer might have helped, but he chose to defend himself. He hoped to use the trial as the stage for a grandiloquent performance, so he could finally get his message across to those for whom he had sacrificed himself, since the steelworkers didn't seem to understand his actions. Some even blamed him for their defeat. A lot of his anarchist comrades were angry at him as well, and wrote articles denouncing him. They claimed that by acting alone he had harmed the entire movement.

But the trial took place sooner than Andrei had expected, and the public was barred from the proceedings. Andrei didn't have time to prepare properly, and none of his intended listeners heard his famous speech. He barely managed to stammer through a few sentences of it. The whole thing didn't even last an hour.

Andrei felt humiliated and robbed. Nothing went as he had planned.

As John C. Kolman erected his buildings around the Pittsburgh prison, he must have had occasion to think of the young man with the revolver. He certainly didn't feel sorry for him. He didn't even feel sorry for his own children, so why should he feel bad for the Russian Jew who had tried to take his life?

Even his beloved daughter Eleanor didn't escape his scorn. He told her she would never get married and would end up a spinster, shuffling around his buildings with a paper bag, collecting rent.

I walk back downtown over Pittsburgh's oldest bridge. It's the oldest steel bridge in the United States, the only one in the city that might still have some trace of Andrei B. stuck to it. In his day, there were railroad tracks leading over it; now they've been replaced by a road and a pedestrian bridge.

I've seen everything I wanted to: the courthouse and the prison, which is still in use, so I wasn't allowed inside. Kolman's opulent architecture.

The house the anarchists used as a base to dig their underground tunnel is no longer standing. Nor is the headquarters of Carnegie Steel, where Andrei B. fired on Kolman.

7

THE WHEELCHAIR SITS AT ONE in a row of tall windows, back facing the door. The white muslin curtain trembles gently. Eleanor, her finger slipped between the two thin strips of fabric, looks out over the sloping green lawn toward the garden shed, which her father had built for her and her brother. Nothing in it has changed: display cases filled with tiny porcelain figures, a table and chairs, her girlhood dolls. The cages Tom used to catch rats and mice are stored away in the attic.

From behind, I can see a white tuft of Eleanor C. Kolman's hair and the folds of a beige blanket wrapped around her. The dining room smells of coffee, dust, old wood, and an amply medicated body.

A nurse in a blue uniform escorts me into the room. Judging from her abruptness, I assume she's the one I spoke with yesterday at the gate. Small and wiry, with short dirty-blond hair and a face I'd forget even if I saw it every day. She gets her name from the virgin goddess Diana.

"Miss Kolman!" Eleanor doesn't stir. "The gentleman is here."

Diana walks to the wheelchair and turns it to face the room. But the old lady is caught on the curtain, the muslin fabric twisting around her like a spiderweb. She yanks at it impatiently, until the nurse succeeds in working her loose, then pushes Diana aside with the back of her hand.

"My glasses!"

Diana obediently pulls a pair of glasses from the pocket of her uniform, places them on the old lady's nose, and retreats into a corner.

The daughter of John C. Kolman looks like a caricature of her father. One of her eyelids droops, probably due to a stroke. The other eye, pale blue, stares straight at me.

I stammer something about how grateful I am to be invited into her home.

Eleanor gestures with her hand toward the fireplace.

There it is, the Bouveret, in the same spot where its original owner hung it a hundred years ago. I have to admit, seeing it in person like this, it has a certain charm. It reminds me of the old color prints of Jesus in a white shirt, radiant head gracefully bowed to his chest, heart bloodied and wrapped in thorns. The figures of the apostles are lost in shadow, the only source of light coming from Jesus and the white loaf of bread he holds broken in his hands. A young girl stands among the men, holding a bowl in her hands. She stands to the left of the Lord, fixing him with a rapturous gaze.

Perched on the mantelpiece beneath the painting are two framed photographs, two children in coffins. Martha, the little rosebud, looks as though she's sleeping, curly hair tied in a bow, her little hands clasped on the blanket, gripping a white rose. The baby boy has sunken cheeks and a mouth like an old man, his eyeballs bulging beneath his waxy eyelids.

"Coffee?"

I'm startled back to my senses. "That would be very nice. Thank you!"

"Diana!"

A column clock, a marble bust of Martha, velvet-bound

photo albums, statuettes, writing implements, an old-fashioned lorgnette. It's as if someone had just set them down for a moment and walked away.

Diana returns with a tray bearing a single cup of thin porcelain tinkling in its saucer.

She pushes Eleanor up to the table. My host doesn't drink coffee, but apparently she'll keep me company.

"Jan van Os." She points to the opposite wall, hung with a rich still life of fruit, flowers, insects, and a mouse feasting on grains of corn.

"Beautiful, really. When did Mr. Kolman acquire it?"

"Eighteen ninety," she says without a moment's hesitation. "Do you see the bee?"

"No."

"Go closer, look more closely." She pronounces each word with great effort, her voice creaking and scraping inside her withered throat. "Not there. On the left! You see?"

Sitting on the exposed red innards of a slightly spoiled fig, sliced open in two, there actually is a little bee.

"Yes, there, I see it now."

"Hooray." Eleanor wheezes.

Diana interjects: "This is a game Miss Kolman used to play as a child. Every morning she would try to find something new about the painting, and if she did, that meant she was going to have a good day. It's been a long time since she's found anything, hasn't it, Ellie? Until this morning. Congratulations on finding the bee! You're going to have good luck today."

"Never mind about that," the old woman says, shooing the nurse back to the corner. She turns again to me. "So you're interested in Bouveret? You're writing a book about him?"

"Yes, that's right."

"He isn't worth it."

"But he's one of the great masters," I stammer. "A successor to Rembrandt, unjustly overlooked."

"It's sheer kitsch. Can't you tell?" Eleanor snaps.

My face flushes red. "But then why . . . I mean . . ."

"Why is it here? For my father's sake, of course. He brought it back from Paris after Martha died. Because of the little girl. He bought a lot of paintings with little girls back then. I wasn't born until much later. Just an add-on." Her chest rattles with laughter, which turns into a cough. Diana steps in with a glass of water and whispers something in her ear.

"Oh, never mind," the old woman says, dismissing her again. "Why shouldn't I talk? It's not like it's going to kill me." She bursts out laughing again, followed by a long bout of coughing. Finally she gasps, "He won't leave me alone. Even now he won't let me be."

"Miss Eleanor," Diana says, raising her voice in an admonishing tone.

"Tom," THE OLD WOMAN SAYS TO ME. "That whole time you left me waiting in the anteroom, and I still wasn't upset. Remember how I assisted you in surgery? What you did to those animals was disgusting, but I didn't mind, just as long as you played with me. Shall we go upstairs?"

She turns to Diana. "We want to go upstairs."

The nurse shakes her head disapprovingly, but she dutifully pushes her out the door. As they pass me, she whispers, "You have to come, too. She thinks you're her brother."

"It's been so long since you've been here. I'm going to show you everything," Eleanor promises as we ride up in the wooden elevator. "I left it all just the way you remember. What took you so long to come back, Tom? Are you still angry? Do you think I stole from you? I would never do that to you, Tom."

Diana pushes the wheelchair down the hall and opens one of the doors. "Our classroom," Eleanor announces with pride. "Remember?"

Bookshelves, blackboard, chalk, glass-doored cabinets stacked with notebooks, maps on the walls, the familiar schoolroom smell.

"Just look at that."

I pick up one of the notebooks. The margins of the carefully ruled pages covered with regular girlish letters are filled with notes scrawled in pencil. I recognize the handwriting of John C. Kolman: "Why isn't the assignment complete? Improve grammar. Excellent!"

She leads me on into Alice's bedroom. There, among the silver hairbrushes and stale bottles of perfume, among the cloudy mirrors, carved deer, and roses, she bursts into tears. A bubbling and gurgling comes from inside her, like water passing through a clogged pipe.

Finally, Diana has a chance to intervene. She pulls a case with a syringe prepared in it out of her pocket. All she has to do is to unwrap it and remove the protective cap. The old woman calms down as the needle plunges into her dried-out skin. She settles back in her chair and closes her eyes.

Diana removes Eleanor's glasses and straightens her covers with an almost loving touch. She beckons me to follow her. Out in the hallway, she presses a button and a bell sounds in another part of the house. A few moments later, a woman appears. I think I spoke to her yesterday, too. A big black woman with a kind round face, she serves under Diana, the shadow of a shadow.

"Put her to bed."

The black woman wheels Eleanor away down a long corridor and turns the corner.

Diana escorts me out.

"I don't know why she agreed to your visit," she says, shaking her head. "I suppose she wanted to talk to someone from the profession. She really does know her art. Years ago, she was working on a book, too, back when I first started here. She would write and write, for hours at a stretch. But she never finished it."

"How long have you been working here?"

"Twenty years."

"That's a long time."

"Yes, very long."

"Do you remember what the book was about?"

"The Italian Renaissance. She asked me to read it. Some of the passages were quite nice. I remember a description of a monastery in Italy. Every cell had a small window looking out on the landscape and a drawing on the wall to go with the view. I can't remember the painter's name."

"Fra Angelico," I say. "I've seen the monastery. It's beautiful."

"There, you see, you've even been there."

"Does Miss Kolman have these episodes often?"

"Not too often." Diana is surprisingly talkative. "But it comes every once in a while. Especially at night. She complains that she wants to die. She cries."

"That's terrible."

"Yes, it's challenging. A few years ago, at one point, she refused to eat. We had to put her on IV. Then somehow she just snapped out of it. Sometimes she gets confused, like she did today with you, and sometimes she talks to ghosts. Usually her father. She complains that he won't let her die, and other things. Some nights it's enough to drive you crazy. She wakes up crying and moaning that she was never good enough for him and he ruined her life."

She suddenly stops. "Why, I shouldn't be telling you this! These are . . . confidential matters. I hope you'll keep it to yourself. I don't even know why I started."

Our brief moment of intimacy has passed and she hastily tells me good-bye.

Outside, I stagger a little, the sandy path crunching beneath my feet.

On the bus ride back to New York, I read through the informational materials I collected on my tour around the Iron City. One of them is a brochure from the Kolman Museum, with a section featuring Eleanor's memories of her father.

"My daddy," she writes, "would have done anything to make me happy. He proved it to me every day in the most loving, intelligent, unusual way. Ever since I was a child, I've felt the strength and gentle protection he provided. He was my fortress."

8

"**H**ERE IT IS."

Professor Kurzweil fishes a yellow Post-it out of a stack of papers and books piled around his computer screen and hands it to me. "Whenever I stick it somewhere, it just falls off anyway."

I make out the name of an archive at the NYU library.

"It's all there," says Kurzweil. "Letters, articles, speeches. Everything Malevich collected." He turns to a young woman sitting at the round table over a cup of tea and a plate of cookies. "Viktor Malevich was the only one in this country who systematically devoted himself to the study of anarchism."

The woman's name is Ilana.

When I called Professor Kurzweil to tell him I was coming, he didn't mention that he wouldn't be alone.

"He did it out of conviction," Kurzweil goes on. "He believed the distorted image of anarchism that most of the public has to this day dates back to political campaigns from the turn of the twentieth century. 'Every good person deep down is an anarchist.' That was Victor's famous dictum. Perhaps you've heard it before?"

Ilana shakes her head.

She's tall and dark, with darting eyes. At first glance nothing special, but after a while I find I can't stop looking at her. I like the way she drinks her tea, warming her cup in her hands like an egg.

She's from Romania and came to the United States on a scholarship two years ago to get her Ph.D. at a private university. She's writing about how Romanian authors collaborated with the fascist and Communist regimes.

"Ilana looked me up a while ago," Kurzweil says, "since I had the honor of knowing Mircea Eliade personally. She wanted a firsthand account of how he viewed his fascist past. I was of no help." He smiles. "But we remained friends. Ilana also shares my interest in psychoanalysis."

I don't know the first thing about psychoanalysis, and I'm always careful not to stray onto that topic with the professor, for fear he'll start throwing names at me like Melanie Klein and Jacques Lacan. At least with Freud or Jung, I might still be able to get by, but even then just enough for a basic exchange.

Fortunately, the conversation moves in a more favorable direction. Ilana talks about the trips she took over the summer, and then we trade insights about New York. She speaks slowly, with a strong accent. When she's searching for a word, she lays a hand on her chest, between her breasts and her Adam's apple. She has long, slender fingers with short-trimmed nails.

Our tourist talk bores the professor. He starts to yawn openly and, not long after that, politely throws us out.

Ilana lives on the East Side and wants to walk home, so I offer to cross the park with her. I store her number in my phone. Even after more than two months in New York, there are only a few people at school I say hello to, and I haven't made any real friends yet. Everyone seems so busy, you have to make plans weeks in advance, even if you just want to get a cup of coffee together. Coming from Prague, where I constantly run into people I know, whether I want to or not, I'm not used to social life being so complicated. At first, I didn't mind spending so much time alone, but a few days ago I decided I needed to change that.

On the corner of Madison and Eighty-sixth, Ilana suddenly comes to a stop. She says I can go back now, that she'll go the rest of the way on her own. But she asks what I'm doing next weekend. Saturday it's Halloween, and she's been invited to a party outside the city, at the country house of one of her university colleagues. She's going to take the train, and suggests I go with her. She asks if I've seen the Hudson Valley yet. We might still catch some fall colors, she says.

JEFF MEYERS HAS WRITTEN SEVERAL BOOKS and runs a creative-writing workshop. His wife, Nina, is an assistant professor in the department of East European studies.

From her father, Nina inherited her Russian surname; from her mother, a house on a lake west of New York. Her parents divorced when she was little and she grew up with her mother. She didn't learn to speak Russian until she was in college, which was also where she met Jeff. Her parents' wedding photos are displayed on top of an old piano, one of the few things her mother didn't get rid of after the divorce.

Jeff and Nina take their partnership seriously. They enjoy telling their friends the story of how they met, and wear their wedding rings with pride. They're planning to have a family.

Nina is a stern woman. She has never forgiven her father for leaving her mother alone, and even though her mother didn't get sick and die until thirty years later, she blames him for that, too. Out of courtesy, she still sees him and his third wife, but she's angry at him. She's angry even now as she pours him a glass of vodka with orange juice.

The elegant gray-haired man with a strong, hooked nose sits on the wooden deck in a chair, watching a white heron search the shallow waters around a little island off the shore of the lake, step by step, so gracefully that it doesn't make even a ripple in the surface.

There are several other guests at the house besides Nina's father and his wife.

As darkness falls, Jeff lights candles in carved pumpkins, and eventually we move inside and sit down at the table to eat. Nina serves shrimp and French cheeses as Vivaldi plays in the background. I know from Ilana that Nina is a bit of a snob, which Jeff tries to balance out by going to pro football games.

Jeff cracks jokes at his students' expense as we sit around the table, and everybody laughs, except for Nina's father, an influential literary critic in his day. "You can't teach talent," he snorts.

"On the other hand, talent only gets you so far," Nina retorts.

"Let's not get into this debate." Jeff offers a conciliatory smile. "It's the same thing every time. Your dad thinks teaching creative writing is useless, that all our graduates do is choke the market with trash, taking up space better left to real writers."

"Am I wrong?" says Nina's father.

"What you leave out is that there's a lot of interest in creative-writing programs. Demand, as you know, creates supply, and far be it from me to turn down work just because some of the students lack talent. How many people actually end up making a living in the field they studied in college? I know an astrophysicist who earns his living as a computer consultant, and a psychologist who works in a PR firm. It's the same thing with writing."

"Aren't you forgetting something? Writing has to have some content, doesn't it? You need to know something first, have some ideas, don't you? Nobody these days knows anything. Students are woefully lacking in education. They don't know how to think. But they can churn out text on any topic, as many pages as you want. I've had a few of these creations come my way, but I wouldn't want to have to read them regularly. Now that's what I call hard-earned bread." Vladimir Semyonovich chuckles at his own joke.

"There's no need to be arrogant," says Jeff.

"There's a certain amount of arrogance that comes with intellect. Thinking people have always held authority. You just aren't old enough to remember. You and Nina have grown up in a world where ideas are for sale. If nobody buys it, it doesn't count. At least you could hide from the Communists, or run away. There's no escaping money. The deformation of commercialism is a voluntary process. It happens inside of people, and its effects are irreversible."

"You know what I think?" Nina interjects. Her voice is trembling. "It's time to say good-bye to bitter, pompous egomaniacs who think they know better than everyone else. People like you and your great idol, Brodsky. Nobody cares about authority anymore. You say there are no more great novels being written, but you just can't see them. You see things only in relation to yourself and your own experience. And you feel unappreciated because no one's interested in your opinions anymore. Why should they be? The world is a lot more diverse than fossils like you could ever imagine."

"Fine, honey, if you say so. I think I've heard more than I care to." Semyonovich deliberately wipes his mouth with a napkin and stands from his chair. He nods to his wife. "Shall we go?"

The two of them leave and Nina walks off and shuts herself in the bedroom for a while. When she reemerges, her eyes are red.

Dinner ends and the other guests gradually take their leave as well. Some of them have cars and offer us a ride back into town, but Jeff and Nina won't let us go. Surely we won't leave them there alone, they say. They ready the guest room upstairs for Ilana and make a bed for me on the couch.

Ilana is dressed for the dinner in a black V-neck sweater, with a bright red smile glued to her face. The more she drinks, the less she talks, unlike Nina, who took off the Vivaldi in favor of Edith Piaf after her father left, and now wants us all to dance.

The fiery eyes of the carved pumpkins stare in at us from the terrace as a dark yellow moon, covered in bruises, slowly rises over the lake.

As the night progressed, the moon was reborn as a bright silver disk shining into the guest room through a crack in the curtains. Ilana's head rested on the pillow, eyes closed. I stroked her long, smooth legs, running my hand lightly over the dark hairs between her thighs. As soon as we were done making love, she closed up and pulled away.

I was awakened by the first flush of a hangover and I heard Ilana crying. Fuzzily, I put together what had happened between us. We both had had a bit too much to drink. But she'd made it clear that she wanted it.

"What's wrong?"

Her back was turned to me, a tangle of dark hair.

"Ilana, what's wrong?"

"Nothing."

"Then why are you crying?"

"I miss him."

"Who?"

"It's none of your business."

"Fine, then, I'll go back downstairs."

IN THE AFTERNOON, BEFORE JEFF DROVE us to the train, Ilana and I took their canoe and paddled out to explore the lake. We spotted a few bald eagles and some gulls, the wind driving a rain of tiny yellow leaves in our faces. Dipping her paddle into the lake at the head of the canoe, Ilana sent green whirlpools spinning back to me in sets of two, and two again.

I tried to ask her a question or two on the train, but she made it clear she didn't want to talk about anything personal. She had closed up like the water's surface.

9

THE PUMPKINS AND SKELETONS have disappeared from the streets, replaced by Thanksgiving decorations. I spend a lot of my time in libraries now.

I found a whole folder on Andrei B. at the archive Professor Kurzweil recommended. Article manuscripts, letters, also copies of a lawsuit he filed against the United States in 1919.

That year, the U.S. government employed a hastily adopted law to deport a group of Russian anarchists from the country. The first ones on the list, of course, were Louise G. and Andrei B.

A lawyer friend of theirs named Jeffrey Weisenkopf filed a suit against the government on their behalf, quoting from the first inaugural address of Thomas Jefferson: "If there be any among us who would wish to dissolve this Union or to change its republican form, let them stand undisturbed as monuments of the safety with which error of opinion may be tolerated where reason is left free to combat it."

They lost the case. The fact that Louise was a U.S. citizen by marriage made no difference.

Just before dawn on Sunday, December 21, 1919, they were hustled aboard the ship, which immediately set sail. Manhattan receded into the distance, the outlines of the skyscrapers with their twinkling lights slowly shrinking in the fog. Louise cried, but Andrei was ebullient. He felt no heaviness leaving the shores of the United States behind. The pendulum had swung back in the other direction. He was eagerly looking forward to the country he had fled like a prison thirty years earlier, but where now he would be able to achieve his dream of freedom.

December 19, two days before they were deported, John C. Kolman died suddenly of cardiac arrest.

The typed originals of Andrei's articles with his edits and corrections are sealed in plastic. But a few yellowed papers have slipped out. Maybe the librarian wasn't careful enough, or was thinking about people like me who need to touch and smell papers; these had the faint scent of cigarette smoke.

Andrei and Louise also typed their letters to each other, the only things they wrote by hand were their closing and signature. The habit of people who write a lot, who make a living by writing: banging out a letter on a typewriter between speeches or articles.

Dear Louise,

Thank you for the news of Germany. Again, I can only repeat what I have already told you in person: The only answer is individual action. Apart from that, I think there is nothing we can do. But is our network . . . capable enough? (I don't think so.) How can we get to that point? I appreciate the efforts to help people in prison, but I believe they are a waste of time.

Michel's essay on the flâneur (and your enthusiastic reaction), frankly speaking, surprised me. This "stroller of city streets," observing everything and intervening directly in nothing, is he not the exact opposite of what we are? Of what we have been our whole lives? Did we not step across that line long ago in our youth? Did we not decide that we would not be reflections, commentators, pocket mirrors, but the hand that intervenes? Did we even have a choice? (A question of compassion, of simple human compassion!)

Who is this "man of the crowd" of whom Michel writes? How does he earn his living? Where does he sleep? Who pays his way? This observation with which he sates himself, while never becoming oversated (or even being at risk of it), is it not a kind of cowardice? What if someone confronts him with a choice? What if they put a brown shirt on him and send him into the streets to beat Jews, what then? What position will he take? Will he simply observe and go with the crowd, or will he stand in opposition? I would like to know.

I view Michel's interest in this romantic "mission" (romanticism isn't a movement, but a need) as a concession to the young friends with whom he surrounds himself. A concession to the times, which he has ceased to understand. To say that modern man is a man without a story!

The observer has no story while he is observing. But is he, too, not part of the monumental tragedy that is taking place, independent of his will? There can be no story without irreversible decisions. I have made some myself, as have you. And the flâneur? If he does not make his decisions himself, someone else will make them for him. And soon! Like it or not, he will be dragged into a story he did not choose.

Perhaps last century, when Baudelaire roamed Paris, there was still time enough for wandering and innocent observation. But now, after the Great War, after the events in Russia, no one is innocent anymore! You cannot just observe, Louise. Monsieur Flâneur belongs to the nineteenth century, not the twentieth. Contemplation in these times is nothing but escape. And to run away now is dangerous.

To ANOTHER UNDATED LETTER, someone had added by hand, "From Louise, Canada, 1940?"

You ask me to remember. I would be more interested in what to do to be able to forget for a while!

I met Andrei B. fifty years ago in New York. I described our meeting in detail in my autobiography and I believe there is nothing to add to it. But apparently you have not read my book. Andrei impressed me with his enormity from the very first time we met. Not in terms of his body. Physically he was rather small. But everything about him was tall and wide; you had to take a deep breath to keep up with him. I myself am from confined circumstances. We grew up counting every potato and walking on tiptoe, speaking in whispers, gathering crumbs. My entire being rebelled against it, against the subservience, the feeling of constant fear that there is a cane over one's head, whether there is one or not. Even before I came to realize (thanks to Andrei) who I was and what was my task in life, I wanted to get away, run away, across the plains, the sea, the ocean, up and away into the clouds, just follow the singing, the noise of the blood wailing in my ears. That was passion. That was Andrei. He never desponded. Not in prison, not in sickness, not in poverty. On some issues I could not agree with him. His analyses were too cold; it bothered me. Ultimately he assessed his own situation with the same cool detachment and decided to end his life. I felt hurt by his decision. And betrayed.

Before the end, there were years in exile. I lived in a small home in the south of France that my friends had bought for me, writing my memoirs. As I finished each chapter I mailed it to the town a few dozen miles away where Andrei had settled with his young lover. We revised the manuscript by letter and over the telephone, a process that was unnecessarily complicated and expensive, and every few days I would try to convince him to come see me. We could work together the way we used to, in the peace and quiet of my home. I could cook for him. He knew how much I liked to cook for him.

He made excuses. No money. He couldn't leave Mimi on her own. Why don't you bring her with you? I asked. She would get in the way of our work, he said. Andrei brought Mimi with him from Berlin. She came from a "good" family. She wanted to marry Andrei more than anything else in the world. Sometimes she threw temper tantrums. She was thirty years younger than him, and hopelessly jealous. Of him, sick and poor as he was.

Andrei had always attracted women. They sensed that with him they could fly free, without any hindrance of pettiness, jealousy, lies. After a while, however, they began to miss the narrow limits they were so accustomed to, and the more uncertain they felt, the more they clung to him. Ultimately they always chose to go back to the cage, which he couldn't even see. There was no way he could understand how tight a grip the claws had on the creature living beside him. How bound they were by the lack of ties.

The other option? Fly free with him as I have. And then lose him.

Only much later, in the final years of Andrei's life, when I had a chance to observe his longest love affair from up close, did I realize that at heart Andrei was the same as any other man. He didn't want a truly free woman by his side, nor did he desire to be truly free himself.

But maybe it takes several generations for the relationship between man and woman, between parents and children, to change, for human beings to begin to love instead of owning, for personal freedom to lead to something other than loneliness and emptiness. We were the first generation to try something like it in practice, and we obviously didn't know how to live by our own ideals. Our instincts were too old-fashioned for our ideas. Our heads pulled us in one direction, our hearts in the other. In every serious relationship I have had, there has come a time when even the most enlightened man has given me the choice: Freedom or me, take your pick. And the men who didn't give me a choice didn't care about me. Maybe they saw me as a mother, a sister, a housemaid, but not a lover. How easily those men left me.

Some wise women, when they get old, prefer women to men.

But that's not what I wanted to write about. You asked about my last conversation with Andrei B., the last time we met.

It was at the morgue. I had requested a moment alone with my oldest friend.

The Mediterranean light streamed in through the round window under the roof, falling across the whitewashed walls. The weight I had felt the past few years suddenly disappeared as the light penetrated everything, making it seem to float. Andrei lay in the open coffin, dressed in his beautiful summer suit.

I stepped toward him. I didn't know what to do at moments like these. How do you say good-bye to the person who matters more to you than anybody else? How do you let go of the love of your life, your most loyal friend and comrade? I put my hand on his forehead. He smiled.

"What game are you trying to play, little girl?"

I pulled back my hand.

"That's better. You don't have to touch me. I'm probably cold and clammy, and I can't feel a thing anyway."

"I don't want to touch you," I said. "I'm mad at you."

"How come?"

"Because you backed out like a coward and left me here alone."

"Now you sound like Mimi."

"Sorry to say, but I'm not that much different from her."

"Emotions are hard. They disguise themselves in all sorts of ways."

"You didn't have to go."

"I don't regret it. I don't like clinging to things that no longer make sense. Like with the McKinley assassination."

"Leave that out of it," I cried. "Why do you have to provoke me now?"

"Louise," he said after a pause. "We didn't agree on most things, did we?"

"That was your obsession," I said. "Actually, we always agreed on the fundamental issues."

"And that was _your_ obsession." He smiled. "In spite of our clashes, though, we stayed together until the end."

"I didn't want to outlive you."

"I'm sorry about that. But what I want to say is that just because you disagree with someone, doesn't mean you don't like them. In fact, you can even love them."

"I know that," I said.

"You see, and I didn't figure it out until just before I died. If I had felt a little better, I would have married Mimi. Don't laugh. It would have made her happy, and it would have been only a slight annoyance to me."

"So what am I supposed to do now?"

"What do you want to do?"

"*The night after you died, I seriously considered ending my life, too,*" I said. "*But it would have been a mistake, I think.*"

"*A big mistake,*" said Andrei. "*Solid material like you. A good woman, and strong. Nothing hurts you, does it?*"

I shook my head.

"*There, you see how lucky you are? You can still do plenty of work.*"

"*That's right,*" I said. "*I'll trim the sail and cruise on, straight ahead. You don't have to worry about me.*"

"*I'm not.*"

"*You know what I was thinking?*"

"*What's that?*"

"*Now that you're dead, I won't think about myself so much anymore.*"

"*I think we've found the best-possible way to be together,*" said Andrei.

I stepped outside into the bright blue and white of day. The undertakers stood in front of the morgue, waiting to close the casket, along with a few friends I had managed to pull together. We set off down the path to the open grave.

I sensed that Andrei was still with me. And he has been with me ever since.

10

JUST BEFORE THANKSGIVING, I came down with the flu. I was sick and alone. I felt sorry for myself and homesick for Prague for the first time since I had left.

The next day, I called Ilana. Apart from her and Professor Kurzweil, I didn't know anyone else well enough to ask for help.

It took a moment before she recognized me on the phone.

She promised to come over and bring me food and medicine. It was dark by the time she arrived. She offered to cook me something to eat, but I couldn't get anything down except yogurt and a few bites of fruit.

She did most of the talking.

She said her favorite writer was Michel Houellebecq. That surprised me. I myself had lost interest in him after his second book. It just felt like he was repeating himself. Not only was his world of depressed adult children, insatiable sex addicts, and money boring, but it didn't seem real to me. As if that was all anyone cared about.

"Oh, really?" said Ilana. "Just look around you. What drives people? What excites them? It might not seem that way from Prague, but Houellebecq's world arrived here in New York a long time ago."

"I think there are plenty of people interested in other things."

"Like what?"

"There are all kinds of alternatives."

"What kinds?" She laughed. "All people care about is their own gratification, that's it. Keeping the desperation at bay."

"So what's your recipe?"

"Recipe?"

"What was your life like before you came to America?"

"I was married ten years," said Ilana. "I've got a child, a son."

"Where is he?"

"With his father. In Germany. His father's German."

Ilana is thirty-four years old.

"How do you say 'thank you' in Romanian?"

"*Mulțumesc.*"

"How about 'love'?"

"*Dragoste.*"

I stayed home for two more days after she visited. I was exhausted by the high fever and coughing. I wasn't even strong enough to walk up and down the stairs. I didn't wash or shave; I just laid under the blanket, listening to the knocking of the heating in the pipes as I stared up at the ceiling. In between bouts of sleep, I reviewed in my mind everything I'd managed to track down so far.

I had promised my parents I'd go home for Christmas, but now I regretted it. It would mean losing two weeks of precious time. A year seems like a long time viewed from Prague, but it really isn't.

A year, for instance, definitely wouldn't be enough for me to feel like I'd actually lived here. For that, I'd have to live through it all at least one more time: the changing of seasons, the local customs. I already knew that once I left, I would long for New York forever. There's no way to comprehend this city, to know it through and through. I long for it and I'm still here.

Desiring the Impossible was also the title of a thick history of anarchism that had been lying next to my bed for several weeks now.

"IT ALL STARTED WITH that Hungarian poet."

We're sitting in a Japanese restaurant on Fourteenth Street, where I invited Ilana for a good-bye dinner. I'm leaving for Prague the day after tomorrow.

"We met in Budapest at a congress organized by the university George Soros set up. I gave a presentation on Romanian literature in exile. There was also a reading by poets, which I missed. Then a party that night. I could tell he was looking at me. I wasn't that attracted to him, but back then, it was enough for me that he was someone new. And that he liked me." She pauses.

"And?"

"I'll never forget the morning after. I got out of bed and pulled back the curtains. Outside, the sun was shining. That movement of opening the curtains was the first free thing I'd done in years. I didn't feel guilty at all. It was like a celebration, from the roots of my hair to the tips of my toes.

"We got together once more after that. I lied to my husband and went to meet him in Timişoara. He came from Budapest, and I rode the train all night to get there. The whole way, the seat underneath me was wet with excitement.

In Timișoara the trees were in bloom. We met at the station at ten in the morning, and we both had to go home the next day at eleven. We got a room in a hotel and made love for twenty-four hours straight, not even going out for food. He offered to leave his wife for me, get a job in construction, whatever, he didn't care. He could baby-sit my son. As I lay there listening to him, suddenly something inside me said, What in the world would I do with you?"

"So you didn't love him?"

"No."

"What about your husband?"

"During those twenty-four hours, I remembered the way it used to be when we were still in love. It didn't last long with the poet. His poems were bad. I had other lovers. I broke up with my husband. Then I came here."

"And now?"

"And now I'm just . . . heartbroken," Ilana says. "I'll never be the same again, I know that for sure."

I pay the check and we step back out onto the street.

Looking at her from the side, she seems a little taller. Taking long strides in her new boots, head tilted backward, marching into the wind. She looks like a woman I've never met.

I pull her into a bar for a drink near my place.

Late at night, on the floor in my room, with all the lights on, Ilana kneels with her torso propped against the unmade bed, moaning.

As I thrust into her drunkenly, I think about the Hungarian poet. I don't mind treating her harshly, especially if she begs for it.

EARLIER THAT AFTERNOON, Ilana and I rode the tramway to Roosevelt Island, formerly known as Blackwell's Island.

We left behind the colorful city lights, the cabin swaying high above the East River's dark surface. Even from that height, we could see the eddies swirling treacherously.

It was a weekday and the island, despite being built up with apartments, was deserted. When we got off the tram, two people boarded the bus with us, but they didn't stay on long, and we rode to the island's northern tip by ourselves.

The air had that hospital smell. I recognized the rotunda from some old photographs. It was all that was left of the famously grim insane asylum that used to be here. A stiff wind blew through the open space between the newer hospital buildings and the park at the island's tip. A week earlier, there had been a light snowfall. There was no longer any sign of it in Manhattan, but the ground here was still covered with a frozen layer. We walked to the lighthouse, built from gray limestone by local prisoners once upon a time.

As we walked back along the western side of the island, the wind now at our backs, we passed the Chapel of the Good Shepherd, once part of the penitentiary complex, which had since disappeared, along with the almshouse and the quarry where convicts were put to work breaking rock. The gutted facade of the smallpox hospital still stands at the island's southern tip, its neo-Gothic turrets covered with ivy. There was also a hospital that specialized in venereal diseases and a home for unwed mothers-to-be.

One other old building stands on the island's southern tip, the country's first pathological laboratory, which also housed a mortuary and autopsy room. In the 1950s, when the buildings around it were knocked down, rumor has it they discovered some old bottles of formaldehyde containing pieces of human bodies.

The penitentiary on Blackwell's Island was a constant threat for the New York anarchists. Andrei B. served his time elsewhere, but Louise G. ended up there with a two-year sentence. Half of it was dismissed for good behavior, at the intercession of her influential New York friends.

During her incarceration, Louise trained to be a nurse and read every book she could get her hands on. She also developed a respect for religion, thanks to a Catholic priest of French origin, who supplied her with literature and met with her in the evenings to discuss what she had read.

"I realized that you don't need to fully share the views of another in order to feel close to him," wrote Louise. "Father Jerome had an enormous capacity for love and compassion. He was humane. I got along better with him than with many of my puritanical anarchist comrades."

Father Jerome also advocated poverty at a time when Protestant preachers were roaming the country, spreading word that it was a man's duty to accumulate wealth. Wealth was a sign of God's blessing, and poverty God's punishment for sins and laziness, they claimed.

"How did money come to be held as the greatest value in the New World?" Louise questioned. "Where does this greed come from, this urge to accumulate more and more? Why are people like bottomless pits that can never be filled?"

Hair, feces, and blood on the operating room tiles. The woman who just gave birth asleep, exhausted, in her bed, a child lying openmouthed on the bed beside her. A purple knot of flesh that isn't going to survive, and even if by some miracle it did, nothing good lies in store for it. Certainly not the love of this worn-out, prematurely aged mother. Who knows how many she squeezed out before this one, how many were born dead, how many she killed or left to die, how many of them are alive without ever knowing anything but hunger.

I heard that in the dustbins of London they find more murdered newborns than dead cats.

The woman sleeps fitfully, her cheeks burning with fever. She's one of the quiet prisoners. Food and pain are the only things she reacts to. If anyone ever gave her a gentle caress, it was so long ago that she has forgotten.

What they call the operating room here is a small room with a sink, a table, and a lamp, separated from the rest of the infirmary by a door. Apart from that, there's just a big walk-through room with sixteen metal beds covered with gray wool blankets, lined up side by side along the plank wood floor. Most of them are occupied. Tied to each bed is a tag stating the patient's name, age, and reason for conviction: Anne Blythe, 23, prostitution. Anne Sullivan, 20, prostitution. Kathy McCormick, 40, theft.

They beg me for alcohol and cigarettes. They pull on my sleeve and whisper, "Get rid of this thing for me! Louise, honey, do it for me. I know you know how. Do it for the little one's sake. Kill him." And they pound on their bulging bellies.

At home, they jump off tables and sit in tubs of boiling water. Knitting needles are even more dangerous. They don't care if they

die having an abortion. At least then they'll have peace, and the
city will look after any children they leave behind.

LOUISE'S CONVICTION—INCITING UNREST—set her apart
from the prostitutes and thieves. As a result, Dr. White
noticed her and offered her a job as an auxiliary nurse. That
meant she was allowed to sleep in the infirmary instead of in
a cramped cell where the water on the walls condensed into
tiny droplets that inched their way down to the floor and she
couldn't read even when she pressed herself up against the
bars, which let in a little daylight.

When he had to operate, Dr. White called in the trained
nurses from Charity Hospital, but for minor procedures—
injections, measuring blood pressure and drawing blood,
emptying chamber pots and wiping sweat, sitting vigil with
the dying and closing their eyelids once they died, changing
bandages and cleaning festering wounds—there was Louise.

After a visit from her highly placed New York friends, the
warden and the prison director began to treat her more kindly,
even allowing her to go on walks sometimes.

I watched the trees slowly wrapping themselves in green, the cur-
rents and eddies within the river's mighty flow, the steamboats'
comings and goings. The sheer curtain of trees on the east bank
thickened with new leaves, partially blocking the view of the
imposing mansions of Ravenswood. I heard the roar of the wind,
the distant train whistle, the clatter of hooves and the rattle of
wheels on pavement. When the wind blew from the west, the

hustle and bustle of the city dominated my hearing, while the easterly wind carried to me the crow of a rooster or the bleating of sheep. Explosions of dynamite boomed from the quarry on the island's southwest side, where the convicts labored breaking rocks.

In June, things slowed down in the infirmary. It was hot and humid, and I opened the windows wide. The nurses at the other hospitals on the island wheeled their patients out to the shaded terraces in their beds and left them there all day. There was always a little breeze blowing above the river's surface, which made the heat just bearable. The penitentiary administration wouldn't allow anything of the sort, however, so the prisoners, even those who were ill, had to remain behind bars.

11

WINTER IN PRAGUE. Fourteen hectic days making the rounds of the pubs. I even got together, briefly, with my ex-wife. She was expecting a baby.

"How come we never had children?" I asked.

She shrugged meaningfully.

She didn't want to talk about us, only about herself and her new husband and her new house outside of Prague, which she would be driving out to in her new car when we were done. She was renting out the flat we used to share, she informed me, dangling the car keys from one of her fingers with the painstakingly polished nails. She didn't drink. No plans of getting a job. She would stay at home with the baby, and then they would have another. They had bought a cottage in the country. Her new man made good money.

"So what about you?" she asked.

"Me? Nothing much."

"How's New York treating you?"

"I've always liked it there."

"Are you seeing anyone?"

I shrugged.

In the morning, before I left, I walked up the hill to the castle to say good-bye. The sun had just struggled its way above the horizon, shaking off the cobwebs of smog, and was rapidly climbing, white and flat. Thin ribbons of smoke wound their way up from the Baroque rooftops of Malá Strana.

Looking down on my hometown, I realized there were some paths I had never figured out, blindly feeling my way to my destination every time. Others I had taken often, but I wasn't sure I could find them again. Trickery and illusions. Stone statues, hundreds of them, lounged and loitered inside niches and next to palace gates. Naked bodies in fresh-fallen snow. I had grown up here among them, but they suddenly seemed excessive. I was looking forward to Manhattan.

SISTER MICHAELA WROTE ME AN E-MAIL, thanking me for my New Year's wishes and asking if I would send her my New York mailing address.

She said she had thought everything through and decided she had nothing to hide.

She was in a completely different place now; she was safe.

"Enclosed space allows the miracle of transformation from a limited earthly life to a life of spirituality, which is the gateway to paradise," Michaela wrote. "Neither the desert nor the celestial sphere, traversed, day by day, by the glowing orb of the sun, will swallow us up. On the contrary, this is the only place where we can stand firm, however lonely it may be. There is only us and God. He hears us and we him."

She wrote that there was a time when she had studied her family's history in detail. In college, she had even begun to write a book about her ancestors, believing that if she retold the past, she would be free of it. Maybe she was right, but her life went in a different direction. She had abandoned the idea of writing a novel and never wrote more than the few pages she was planning to send me.

She said she still didn't understand quite what I was after, but nevertheless she would send me her notes. They didn't concern her anymore.

"There's still one piece of information I owe you," Michaela wrote. "In New York, you asked if there was ever any talk in our family about the assassination attempt. I said no, but that isn't true. My aunt once told me when the gun was pointed at my great-grandfather Kolman's heart, he suddenly had a vision of Martha. She was standing beneath the window in a pool of sunlight. She was wearing a white dress and was looking straight at my great-grandfather, smiling."

On January 5, when I got home (taking the liberty of calling New York my home), I found an envelope from Sister Michaela waiting in my mailbox. A stack of neatly typed pages from the precomputer age. They gave off a strangely sweet aroma. This must be how the desert smells, I thought.

Alice

Alice, the nanny, and the maid are getting the children dressed. Four-year-old Tom has on pants, socks, and shoes, as well as a shirt and a vest, but he's racing around the cabin, slipping away from the nanny as she chases after him with his coat and scarf. He wants to go outside as is. Three-year-old Martha, whom the women have finally managed to get dressed, starts taking off her clothes again, whining that she's going to be too hot in her coat.

Alice is uneasy, and Tom is trying her patience, almost as if he can sense it. He doesn't listen to her until she starts shouting at him and threatening him with a switch. Finally, both he and Martha allow themselves to be buttoned into their navy blue sailor's coats so they can go out for a short walk before breakfast. Tom runs ahead, followed by Alice, holding Martha's hand. The nanny goes with them, while the maid stays behind in the cabin to tidy up after the children and supervise the maids from the shipping company when they come to do the morning cleaning.

The Atlantic is calm today. Morning sun floods the upper deck. The shoreline has long since disappeared, just a rolling mass of water stretching as far as the horizon, swallowing up the summer sky. Gulls hover in a sparkling tail at the rear of the ship.

Alice had traveled to Europe before she was married, with her parents and sister, but ever since the wedding she had been too busy to make it over the ocean. First, furnishing their home, then Tom was born, then Martha. In the winter, she didn't feel like going anywhere with the children, and they spent their summer months at a private club on Lake Conemaugh, where the Pittsburgh businessmen and their families got together to fish, hunt deer, race sailboats, make business deals, and clear their lungs of the city's filthy air.

It's the children's first time on an ocean liner. Tom pleads to be taken to the captain's bridge and engine room, and Martha's eyes bulge on seeing the endless stretch of water.

On deck, they run into some friends they were socializing with after dinner the night before, and Tom and Martha beg to play with their children for a while. Alice leaves them with the nanny and goes off in search of her husband. She looks in the café, the day lounge, and the smoking room before finally checking the library, an oval room with tables and cushioned chairs, bathed in the morning light that filters in through a cupola of frosted glass. John C., hidden behind a wooden replica of a Doric column, sits lost in thought at one of the tables. Actually, he is halfway reclined in a low upholstered armchair, legs crossed, chin jutting out belligerently. A stack of newspapers sits piled before him, but he isn't reading. His blue eyes are fixed on the ornately carved ceiling. He must have gotten hold of the papers yesterday evening before their departure. Alice glances at the front page of the newspaper on top: Murder by negligence; club guilty, not God.

She is a bit nearsighted, so she has to bend down. The caricature, printed in color, shows a group of powerful men from Pittsburgh, including her husband. He is on the grass, half-sitting, half-reclining, as he is now, giving an impish look at Carnegie, who squats on a cliff overlooking a lake, holding a fishing rod, with a canvas fishing hat on his head. His young business associate Knox stands fawningly at his side. Alice recognizes most of the faces in the cartoon. They are friends of her husband; she and their wives play bridge together, organize charity events and musical soirées. She has danced with these men at lamplit parties on Lake Conemaugh. In the picture, holding fishing rods and glasses of champagne, they drink a jubilant toast as a dam crumbles beneath their feet, streams of water spurting out.

"Who do they think they are?" Alice exclaims. "You should sue them."

"They don't name anyone."

"But it's obvious it's you."

John C. shrugs. "They can't prove a thing on us."

"What is there to prove? It's nobody's fault it rained."

"Let's go have breakfast," her husband says abruptly.

He folds the newspaper into his dark leather briefcase, which normally he entrusts to his secretary, George. But just to be safe, this time George remained in Pittsburgh. John C. has friends, but they all belong to the club, and he has no doubt that when push comes to shove, it will be every man for himself. He would do no differently. The only person he can count on to be loyal is George, whose salary he pays. He goes to ring for a steward to carry his briefcase back to the cabin, but Alice insists on taking it herself. She accompanies her husband up to the deck, then leaves him and heads to the first-class section. Inside the cabin, she sits down at the desk and pulls out the newspaper.

The number of deaths had already been estimated at over two thousand people. Many of them were still missing, probably carried dozens of miles away by the water. Nothing was left of the town that lay fifteen miles downstream except the Methodist church, the firehouse, and a few homes that were miraculously spared. The old stone bridge was also still standing. Shortly after the flood, a fire broke out amid the avalanche of debris, mud, and human and animal corpses that piled up at the bridge as the most devastating wave swept through the town. The fire burned for three days. People said they could hear the cries of survivors trapped beneath the wreckage.

The Chicago Herald *carried stories of the people who survived:*

> *Anna Fenn, Acacia Street: Before the flood hit, Anna's husband, John Fenn, went to help the neighbors carry their furniture up to the second floor. The wave swept their home away moments before it flooded the Fenns' house, where Anna remained with their seven children: John Fulton (12), Daisy (10), Genevieve (9), George Washington (8), Virginia (5), Bismarck S. (3), Esther (1½). Mrs. Fenn held the youngest child in her arms while the others huddled close to her. She described the*

scene as follows: "The water kept rising and lifting us up, till we hit our heads on the ceiling. It was dark and the house was shaking; you couldn't breathe. I don't know for sure when my children gave up the fight for life and drowned, one after the other. I can't put into words the suffering I felt with the bodies of my seven children floating around me in the dark." Mrs. Fenn's husband, stove maker John Fenn, also failed to survive the flood. Mrs. Fenn is soon expecting the birth of her eighth child."

Alice thought there might be a way for her to help Mrs. Fenn and her eighth child. But John C. strictly forbade her from getting involved in anything related to the flood. "We've got to be careful," he said. "Any overly personal assistance on our part could end up being turned against us." The Fishing and Hunting Club formed a relief committee. About half the members contributed several thousand dollars each, and they also sent a thousand woolen blankets to the town. But they played innocent, refusing any direct responsibility for the disaster and not responding to the attacks on them in the papers. The method proved to be effective.

Alice reads that, shortly after the flood, a group of town residents attacked one of the club's cottages in revenge, but there was nobody there, since the few members who decided to spend that May weekend at the lake had left to return to the city before the misfortune struck. The only ones there were the caretaker of the property and a fisheries agent, who with a team of twenty Italian workmen were digging spillways up until the last moment to try to relieve the pressure, and piling mud and rock on the dam to strengthen it. When they saw that it was futile, they sent a *telegram warning the town that it was in danger, and fled. The body of the telegraph operator Bertha Altman, who received the alert, has not yet been found. All that remained of her in the ruins of the station were the metal frames of her glasses.*

The attackers, seized with impotent rage, broke into the club-house dining room, smashed a few plates, and moved on.

Alice reads that the flood was caused by the spring thaw in the Appalachian Mountains, three days of heavy rain, a lack of maintenance on the dam, and, above all, incompetent modifications to the dam, lowering it for the construction of a carriageway across it. "The responsibility lies with the owners of the lake, the members of the Fishing and Hunting Club. But these men rank among the powerful of this country, who apparently cannot be held to answer for anything, not even the death of thousands of people."

Mornings on the lake had always been the most beautiful. The surrounding woods were filled with birds singing, and it was so lovely having coffee served on the veranda. The children were able to run around in the fresh air, far away from the blast furnaces of the steel mills, the chimneys spewing smoke and ash over the city day and night. Now all that was left of the lake was a muddy crater with the original bed of the Conemaugh River winding along its bottom.

The ocean was calm throughout the voyage. They made it to Liverpool in seven days. John C. wanted to stay in London, but Alice was eager to see Paris, so she decided to go ahead and take the children with her. They stayed at the Hotel Belle Europe.

While he was in London, John C. met with art dealers, exchanged telegrams with George about the situation in

Pittsburgh, and studied the Wallace Collection of paintings in detail. He also bought a new set of undergarments and a tuxedo. Meanwhile, in Paris, Alice had two dresses sewn at the internationally renowned House of Worth: an ivory-colored ball gown of silk, decorated with lace and silver threads, and an afternoon gown in a warm red-brown shade. Princess Metternich was said to have ordered a similar dress the same year for her autumn strolls through Vienna.

I think that the spring of 1889, when the flood swept Johnstown away, was the last time my great-grandmother Alice felt young. As if the Johnstown disaster put a curse on the family.

At night, she sometimes dreamed that she was Anna Fenn. Gasping for breath, groping about in the wet and dark, her fingers brushing up against cold objects, terrified to the point that she awoke with a loud scream, and the only thing that would calm her down was a spoonful of the laudanum she kept by her bedside.

She wanted to love her husband and bear him children. She hadn't expected to be punished for it.

Once, after Martha died, she secretly went to visit the flooded town. She took the train part of the way, but she didn't dare set foot inside the local station, so she hired a coach instead. It had been exactly two years since the flood, and the whole region was coming back to life. The repaired steelworks was up and running, a new library was being built, and the wooden houses had a fresh coat of paint. Young trees lined the waterfront. They had managed to clear away all the wreckage, and the only reminder left in places was the sweetish smell of river mud.

Alice didn't step out of the carriage, for fear she might be recognized. She sent the driver to ask where the Fenns lived, but he came back empty-handed. The only member of the stove maker's family still alive was Anna, but she had moved away.

Alice made him go back and ask in depth about everything. After Anna's eighth child was stillborn, she had gone to live with her relatives in Virginia, and had stayed there ever since. She got remarried and her name was Maxwell now. Or something like that.

Alice told the driver to take her to the cemetery. The white slabs of the tombstones stretched to the horizon. Somewhere among them were the graves of the eight dead children of Anna Fenn. There were also seven hundred nameless flood victims buried here, who were never identified.

She remembers the letters her mother sent to the East Coast hotels where she spent her honeymoon trip. The delicate envelopes faithfully awaiting her every morning to take into her warm bed and read over morning coffee while John C. perused the mail and leafed through the daily papers. At the end of each letter, Alice's mother begged her not to show them to her husband, embarrassed at her flowing, spidery handwriting and at how banal the contents seemed to her: "We miss you so much. I hope you will come see us as often as possible. You could spend your days with us and have Mr. K. pick you up on his way home from work and stay for tea—it would give us the feeling of having the family back together again."

"Tell Mr. K. the Japanese vases are magnificent. We are much obliged for his gifts."

In one of the letters, in between bits of gossip from home, it said, "Submit to your husband's will in all things."

But I can't when it comes to this, Alice argues now with her dead mother.

You must!

Alice stops the maid as she prepares to serve the soup. She'll do it herself. Today is the last time the whole family will eat lunch together. She stands, picks up the ladle, dips it into the serving dish, and reaches for her husband's bowl, expecting him to hand it to her. But John C. ignores her. Leaning in toward their daughter, he whispers something in her ear, and Ellie bursts out in laughter. Tom absentmindedly fiddles with his silverware. Alice stands a moment, ladle in hand, arm outstretched toward her husband. Finally she lets go of the ladle, splattering soup on her clothes, and John C. lifts his head. Tom squirms, expecting the usual scene to transpire. His mother will burst into tears, then make a rapid exit. But this time it's different. Alice's legs give way and she drops to the ground without a word. The servants come racing in and carry her up to bed. Nobody panics. But the incident confirms John C.'s belief that, despite his wife's objections, Tom needs to get out of the house as soon as possible.

The next morning Tom's father drove him to the station, and from there they continued on first-class to Cambridge, where the boy was entering boarding school. From Cambridge, John C. Kolman traveled directly to New York, boarded a ship, and sailed to Europe. He stayed three months. While he was away, his secretary, George, sent him detailed reports on everything happening at home.

For several weeks after her husband's and son's departure, Alice withdrew behind the heavy drapes of her bedroom, writing Tom letters filled with instructions on how he should behave to avoid colds, tuberculosis, pneumonia, and all the other illnesses that could easily kill a twelve-year-old boy living far from home. She cried the whole day through, imagining her son with no one to ensure that he didn't go outdoors without a hat and that he drank his daily two glasses of milk. The nanny took care of Ellie, who was two. Sometimes Alice would call her daughter to come to her bedside, but she would quickly send her away again when Ellie's babbling got on her nerves.

When she finally left her room, it was November. As George wrote John C., "She keeps herself busy cleaning and tidying up the house, but I think there are times she overdoes it and then she's extremely tired." Someone had to supervise the maids as they remade the house for winter, taking down and washing the summer curtains, and hanging up the winter tapestries stored in chests over the summer. Cleaning the carpets and upholstery, and removing the dust that had accumulated on the fabric wallpaper over the summer.

After she lost Tom, she stopped sleeping with her husband. She didn't want any more children. Withdrawing into herself, she tended only to her dressing gowns and rose beds. Outwardly, she remained calm, but it was a calm dependent on the bottle of laudanum she kept by the side of her bed.

She was thirty-five. In photos from that time, she is even more beautiful than when she got married. She refused to pose, instead sitting casually, looking directly into the lens. Her soft white shoulders and neck stand out against the black fabric of her low-cut dress, her arms crossed on her chest. No smile. Her dark eyes, elongated toward the temples, have an absent look, giving the slight impression of vacuousness.

The furnishing of their new estate on the Atlantic coast took place without her involvement, as did the construction of their residence in New York. Her body relocated, but in her mind she was elsewhere. At around fifty, she stopped walking and had to be carried in a wheelchair. To walk upright required more will than she possessed.

Or I could be wrong and everything my great-grandmother Alice did was in fact evidence of a healthy desire to survive. With her mental vacancy, her tincture of opium, and her confinement to the wheelchair, she carved out a space for herself where her husband could not get at her; his aggression was confined to comments over meals. Even during his bouts of arthritis, she no longer had to sit by his bed and change his compresses. Ellie did it instead.

Alice became noticeably livelier after Kolman's death. She began to take pleasure in food again, and in flowers, too. Nothing made her happier than saving money. She maintained an active correspondence with all their contractors and battled with them over every cent. It was like a sort of revenge on John. He bought presidents and she, his wife, argued over small change. Her small, belated rebellion.

In the days shortly before her death, she was childlike, almost happy. She rose to the surface and stayed there, among the small pleasures. The sky was as blue as it had been in the days of her childhood, and anything too painful remained far away, separated from her by a layer of time and opium.

Eleanor

My great-grandfather John C. Kolman died on Friday, December 19, 1919, of a heart attack. He died in the second-floor bedroom of his New York residence, at the top of a dark wood-paneled staircase.

On Thursday evening, he had gone down to the parlor and sat in the green easy chair in front of the fireplace, looking at his favorite painting, El Greco's Saint Jerome. *It reminded him of his grandfather Solomon, whose liquor store had been his school. He started working there when he was just a child, then struck out on his own, went into the coal business, and by the age of thirty had made his first million.*

Kolman was pleased with himself. Any feelings of guilt he had had been washed away by his daughter's death. Martha's suffering had redeemed him, but he must never forget it!

When Ellie was five, he gave her a locket with a picture of Martha and a ringlet of her golden hair. He made her wear it around her neck all the time, and checked often to make sure she had it on.

On Thursday evening, he sat on the sofa in the parlor, savoring his collection. The tableaux stood out clearly against the darkness, thanks to the ring of electrical lighting that he had had installed. It was expensive, but worth it. The oil paints came alive. If anyone had told him that tomorrow at this time he would be upstairs croaking in his bedroom, he would have laughed. His parents had lived to be over eighty, and he wasn't even seventy yet. He still had big plans.

Eleanor sat in the parlor with him, waiting patiently until he got tired and asked to be taken back to bed, where he had spent the last fortnight battling off a cold. He berated her in the elevator, and refused to take his medicine before he went to bed. Their bedrooms were next to each other, and John C. insisted that she *leave the door open. He would call out to her several times a night. There were moments when she grew tired of his moodiness.*

When it came to business negotiations, John C. Kolman generally remained silent. His art supplier Duveen complained: A man could talk himself to death and still not know where he stood. Kolman would just listen quietly, with no telltale facial expression to give away what he was thinking. He would sit through several meetings that way before he decided to try out a painting or sculpture. He always took things on a trial basis, taking his time. He knew he could afford to. Duveen doted on him. But once Kolman was convinced of the merits of a purchase, he would dispense of tens, even hundreds, of thousands of dollars with a wave of the hand.

John C. Kolman was a crafty man. Even as a youth, he understood the power of silence, leaving him with all the trumps, while his opponent voluntarily gave up his. It was part of his strategy to keep the enemy guessing. And everyone was his enemy.

Enemies could be bought, too.

For her fifteenth birthday, Eleanor got a diamond ring from him, which made her burst into tears, because it looked like an engagement ring. When she decided, eight years later, at the end of World War I, to go to Europe with the Red Cross, her father financed the field hospital where she worked, and on her return he held a celebration, pinning a medal for bravery on her: a brooch in the shape of an American eagle, encrusted with red rubies, blue sapphires, and diamonds.

When in the fall of 1919 he refused yet another request for her hand in marriage, he gave her a triple strand of pearls and took her on a trip to Egypt.

A messenger brought the pearls together with a huge bouquet—white roses with a tiny envelope tucked inside them: "Another offer of marriage today. I threw that nonsense straight in the trash. You're getting too popular! Hope you're thinking of me. J. C."

She burst into tears. She had been sure the package, bouquet, and message were from someone else.

Normally, her father used monogrammed envelopes, but this one was solid white. Did he do it on purpose to deceive her? Would her daddy intentionally hurt her?

There are photos of John C. kissing little Ellie on the mouth and photos of her as an adult with her father's hand resting possessively on her knee.

Her father had even gone so far as to pay off her last suitor, a young doctor who refused to give Eleanor up. Kolman offered the doctor a sum too large to resist. He set up his own practice and married another girl. Eleanor thought it was strange that he disappeared so suddenly, without a word of explanation. But since she was young and had no experience with men, and since she was waiting for her first true love but had no idea what that would actually look like, she didn't bother to dig into what had happened to him.

Ever since she was little, her father had taken her to Europe. She took part in all his business ventures. He took her opinions seriously, and although he wouldn't send her to college (he wasn't in favor of public education for women), he enabled her to gain an exceptionally wide perspective. He appreciated her business acumen and regretted that she hadn't been born a boy.

Tom (my grandfather), in his opinion, was useless.

How proud he was, how proudly he laughed, when he found out his four-year-old girl was secretly selling the moralistic pictures they handed out to children in church!

My great-grandfather Kolman knew only one kind of happiness: the happiness of winning.

When things were going his way, Eleanor was floating on air. She was his princess, and he laid the whole world at her feet.

But he had his bad moments, too, and when he did, he would knock Eleanor down from the heights with such cruelty that it baffled her. She sensed only that her daddy was suffering and so suffered along with him.

Her father had always made it clear that she was special. At meals, he made her sit across from him, leaving her mother to take one of the seats normally reserved for children. Whenever they had a visitor who asked to see his collection, Eleanor was the one who would accompany him. When they were in Pittsburgh, he would take her for walks to Martha's grave and back on a regular basis. Along the way, they would discuss whatever Kolman had on his mind, and as a result, Eleanor knew more about his affairs than anyone else.

What Kolman failed to achieve in his lifetime, he accomplished with his death.

After the nervous breakdowns and suicide attempts, a state of lethargy ensued. Eleanor refused to eat. She wouldn't even move, just lying quietly, tears streaming down her cheeks.

After the tears dried up, she entered the final stage of

mourning: the daily small-scale work of preserving her father's memory forever.

While he was still alive, she was able to be critical of him. They had different opinions on politics, especially on women's issues. After his death, she became completely at one with him.

Eleanor became one of the richest unmarried women in America. Her mother was still entitled to the use of all three homes and a lifelong annuity. Her brother got the house on Long Island, where he lived with his wife and children, and a little bit of money, but everything else went to Eleanor, according to Kolman's will. Crafty as he was, Kolman knew the only property he would never have to part with was the property he left to Eleanor. His daughter would take good care of it for him.

Eleanor didn't want to stay in the New York residence alone with her mother, so she bought a country villa with land along the Hudson River and moved her belongings there. From then on, she went to New York only to visit. She slept in the guest room, since her father's bedroom and hers were both locked shut after his death. But first she had his heavy deathbed, carved of walnut, placed next to her own.

For twelve years, until Alice died, the two beds stood side by side, fully made, behind the drawn green curtains. It wasn't until my great-aunt Eleanor was rid of her mother, of her blame and accusations, that she was able to fully devote herself to the memory of John C.

During the house's transformation into the publicly accessible Kolman Museum, Eleanor had the bedrooms reopened. She had the carpenters dismantle the beds, tear out the dark wood *paneling, rip out the door frames, and incorporate them all into the newly built reference library.*

Eleanor took the door that connected the two bedrooms and used it as the door to her study. It still opened and closed with the same unmistakable creak her father used to complain about with a smile.

No man could ever make her feel as special as he had. She mustn't allow the living to threaten the dead. She mustn't betray her father.

Of course she had yearnings. Between thirty and forty, she had longed to have children. But even in death, her father demanded everything of her, so she had a dog instead. Later, during World War II, she took in some teenage girls who had been left homeless by the bombing in London, and she continued to act as their fairy-tale aunt for long after the war.

She also fell in love a few times. They were all older men: first the chairman of the board for the Kolman Museum, then a professor of art history she had appointed as director of the collection, and, finally, her personal physician. None of them ever knew how Eleanor truly felt. They interpreted her mood swings as an old maid's typical irritability, which nobody wants to take a close look at, for fear of what they might find: the embryos smothered before they could be conceived, the soulless baby birds stuffed behind the walnut headboard.

One day, my great-aunt Eleanor returned to Pittsburgh and the family home, with its green lawns in view of the cemetery in the woods. The house that, for decades, despite the family's absence, had been kept up by three maids, a caretaker, and a gardener. Nobody there remembered John C. Kolman or my great-grandmother Alice anymore.

The resident staff had grown old and passed away. The only one who wouldn't die was Eleanor, who had been waiting for death a good ten or twenty years. At a certain point, she let go of the rope, surrendering to the murmurs and smells of yesteryear, letting herself be swept along by the current. She started talking to her childhood governess and her brother Tom, waiting outside the bedroom door for her mother to call her in. She went on pony rides, made tea for her dolls. Sunlight and birdsong streamed in through the windows of the garden shed. Even from across the meadow she could see the green treetops of the Kolman woods shaking under the surge of wings. Everything was big, vibrant, and full of life.

She sits on her father's lap, stroking his graying hair and close-trimmed beard.

"Look in my eyes. Who do you see there?"

"I don't know," says little Ellie, feeling embarrassed.

"You." Her father smiles. "You're my one and only little girl now. Tell me you'll always be as good as Martha. Will you always love your daddy? Rosebud died and Daddy doesn't have any other little girl."

Ellie sobs, wrapping her arms around her father's neck. She feels so sorry for him that she thinks her heart is going to break.

When she was ninety years old, she invited me, her great-niece, Eleanor Louise Kolman, to Pittsburgh. I went to visit her often anyway, but this was a special invitation.

Of all the relatives, she liked me best, and it wasn't because of my name. In fact she had always hated her name; it struck her as unfeminine. When she was young, I was told, she had considered changing it to Margaret or Lily.

When my parents named me Eleanor, she didn't speak to them for months. She suspected my grandfather Tom of having suggested it to his son in the hopes that it would make my father's childless aunt turn sentimental and leave everything to her namesake. I was told that for a long time she wouldn't even visit them to look at me.

Gradually, though, she grew fond of me. I had always liked paintings, and my great-aunt started walking me through the collection, showing me this and that. She paid attention to how I reacted. Then she took me to Europe with her. I was only eleven when we went to Italy, but my great-aunt and I almost always agreed about what we should see.

We went together to the Dominican Convent of San Marco in Florence, where my great-aunt fell in love with the murals of Fra Angelico all over again. When we got back, she began to write a book about them.

She invited me to Pittsburgh to explain her plan to me. There was no doubt in her mind that I would agree to it. After all, she was going to make me rich. Maybe not the richest unmarried woman in America, as she had once been, but still, extremely rich. The Kolman collection was increasing in value every year.

Along with her wealth, of course, I would be taking on a burden, but she had been preparing me for it ever since I was a child.

We sat down to tea in the drawing room and I told my aunt about the university. Her influence was visible in that respect as well. I had chosen art history as my major.

Then she asked me to help her unclasp the necklace with the locket containing Martha's likeness. I went to hand it to her, but she shook her head.

"It's yours," she said. She told me her plan.

I set the locket down on the table. "I can't."

"What are you saying?"

"I'm sorry."

"You might change your mind."

"No."

"Why not?"

What was I supposed to say? That I detest the very air in the house where I grew up? The cold loneliness that comes with money? That I'm troubled by my family's past? That I feel personally guilty?

I was still a little girl when my aunt and I traveled around Europe. It was all like a fairy tale. A lot had changed since then.

"But why, Ellie? Why can't you just let me die in peace?"

It was my secret. I hadn't told anyone yet. But what could I do at that moment? "Because I want to enter the convent," I said, "that's why."

Dear heaven, break open and shower her! Pain, torture her no more. All that she missed out on. All that will never come back. Bury it all in ruins, you blue, bluer than blue sky, arching like her father's Chinese bowl over the meadow of her childhood; bury her, the girl on a pony, the girl with the locket pressed, wedged deep into her chest.

Daddy, screams the wounded Eleanor, she's rejecting you!

I WROTE SISTER MICHAELA A LETTER thanking her.

I slipped her notes inside the cover of Josef's notebook,

which I had brought to New York with me. Now, besides Josef's unfinished novel, the blue envelope labeled ANARCHIST also contains copies of Alice Kolman's letters and the papers of Andrei and Louise that I managed to get from the archive. I'm not sure yet what I'm going to do with it all.

A hundred-some-year-old little girl who can't die.

I was reminded of Eleanor C. Kolman in the plane back to New York from Prague. There was a woman on the flight, probably crazy or a junkie in withdrawal. She was wearing a knit beret like the kind my grandmother Týna wore, with dark sunglasses hiding her face. She was holding her large white hands out in front of her, as if they didn't belong to her, and her wrists were wrapped in bandages. Somewhere over Canada, she decided she wanted to jump out of the plane. She got in a fight with the flight attendants, howling like a soul in purgatory. Finally, they had to handcuff her, and once we landed at the airport, the police took her away.

Like Eleanor, she kept calling for her father, begging him to forgive her.

12

ILANA DIDN'T RESPOND TO MY E-MAILS from Prague. She wrote back only once, to say that New York was buried in snow. The city had been totally quiet for two days, she said. Also, she had started going to group therapy.

I called her a few days after I got in, and she invited me over for dinner.

She lived in one of the old, well-preserved buildings near the university. Arriving there, I climbed the narrow stairway to the fourth floor and found the door to Ilana's apartment propped open. A deep voice and laughter echoed down the corridor.

A guy stood with his arms outstretched, hanging off the door frame to the kitchen, where Ilana was apparently making food. His feet were crossed and his ass stuck out into the entryway.

His presence irritated me right away, along with his foreign-sounding Romanian and sloppy green shirt.

It was too late to turn around, though. Ilana came out of the kitchen and gave me a kiss on both cheeks.

The guy turned to me with a full black beard and a smile, holding out his pawlike hand. "Hi, I'm Marius."

Ilana was wearing a clingy navy blue T-shirt with a low neckline and a tight black skirt. She looked thinner than I remembered. She had her hair pulled back in a ponytail, with a silver chain around her neck and a red smile painted on her lips.

"Marius lives in Oregon, but he's here at an arts center outside New York on a three-month scholarship. Can you believe it? He's an old friend. We went to high school together."

She clasped her arms around his waist as she spoke.

The apartment was small and dark. In one corner, there was still a stack of moving boxes. In another, there was a travel backpack, which was definitely not Ilana's.

I noticed a piece of dark velvet hanging on the wall, with rows of earrings stuck in it, each one missing its partner.

"There was this period where I just kept finding lost earrings," Ilana explained. "So I started collecting them, just for fun. Sort of like a diary. I still remember where I found every one."

"I didn't realize you had artistic ambitions." I could hear how silly the word *ambitions* sounded.

"I don't," she said. "I just felt like it."

"You did some nice things back in high school," said Marius. "I remember. You used to make jewelry, and clothes, too. Some of it was pretty wild."

"I made them because there weren't any to buy," said Ilana.

"Remember that time you recited your poems at the school assembly?"

Ilana gave a loud laugh. "That was embarrassing!"

"It was awesome! I can still see it. After all these neatly groomed little kids with slicked-back hair singing cute little songs, this beautiful, fragile girl walks onstage in a long black dress with bare shoulders—"

"Stop, please!"

"—and starts reciting erotic poems."

"They were not erotic!"

"They were ecstatic," said Marius. "I remember it well, not to mention that you gave me the poems to read later on. About how the sea was entering you, and you were dissolving, about your skin and your hair and your lips, and looking at yourself naked in the mirror. . . ."

"How do you remember all that? It was so stupid."

"I was in love." The big bear shrugged.

"Here, I brought some wine," I said.

"So stupid," Ilana repeated, handing me a full glass. "Cheers."

"Do you still write poems?" I asked quietly.

"No," she said. "Luckily, I found out in time that I'm much stronger on theory."

"So you're from Prague?" said Marius. "I was there once. Everyone says what a beautiful city it is, but I think it's awful. All those fancy facades and bright colors. It's like Disneyland. Plus all the rabbis and golems. I wouldn't be able to do anything there. I need space. I don't care if the buildings are ugly, as long as I can see the sky. Berlin, now that's a cool city. And it was even better before they started building it up. Or Sarajevo. Ever been there? Even nasty old Bucharest is better than Prague. You know what's a shame? That they didn't drop more bombs on you guys during the war. That would have cleared it out a bit. So what are you interested in anyway, if you don't mind my asking?"

"Why would I mind?" This guy was obnoxious. I didn't understand why Ilana had put me in this situation. "I'm a historian, but I'm actually more interested in the future. I feel like

New York is sort of an observation tower. You climb up and you can see a long ways, maybe even to the end of the world."

Marius snorted. "Everyone's going on about the end of the world these days."

"Who's everyone?"

"Philosophers, environmentalists, artists. Everyone. It's all the rage. If you want to make a career for yourself, just babble on about catastrophe and mix in a little Lacan, some Derrida, a drop of Levinas, and a dash of Heidegger. Marx isn't so popular anymore, but you can't make do without him. Nobody yet's done a better job of describing the shit of capitalism. But don't even mention Lenin. You won't get tenure with him. Better off using Benjamin—you can slip him in anywhere. The only one with the balls to say how things really are, in my opinion, is Žižek. All of these protests and activists and resistance movements and neoanarchists are just impotent stooges. All they do is moralize. Which is exactly what the powers that be need: moderate resistance within the bounds of the law. It gives them an alibi."

"So what do you suggest?"

"What Žižek says. Seize control of the state and use it to change its own mechanisms. Activists always talk about change from the bottom up, but it isn't going to happen. It never has and never will. Every revolution has started by overthrowing the state."

"Revolution?"

"You think it's funny?" Marius got up, went to the entryway, and dug around in his coat pocket. A moment later, he came back with a pack of cigarettes. "Mind if I light up?" Neither one of us was a smoker, but Ilana handed him an ashtray.

"Why do you think it's funny, if you don't mind my asking?"

"I don't know. Who said I did?"

"You smirked, didn't you?"

Ilana interrupted. "I just read an interesting book. It's by an environmentalist who argues that the difference isn't so much between people in favor of violent change and people who reject it as between people who do something and people who do nothing."

"If you ask me, violence is inevitable." Marius nodded. "Unfortunately. The people who are in power are never going to give it up voluntarily. Nothing changes that way. You want to fight by writing petitions? Buying organic carrots? Recycling?"

"What do you do?"

He shrugged. "So far, I just paint. I humbly and shamefully confess I'm not blowing up dams or gunning down the heads of multinational corporations, even if they deserve it even more than the politicians they have eating out of their hands. I'm a painter. And I even admit, in my sunnier moments, I'm pretty happy with where I'm at. I'm not stuck in some stuffy academic department. I've got my independence. I get by the best I can, out on the street, in the mud and rain, like a dog. But it suits me. I need to feel things up close. Fight for them."

What a clown, I thought to myself. "Didn't you say you were here on some prestigious scholarship?"

Marius didn't respond. Just ran a hand over the scruff on his face, smoking and staring up at the ceiling.

"But I do think," he said, suddenly snapping back to life, "that my peaceful days are over. When it comes to some things, art just isn't enough."

Ilana opened another bottle of wine. We hadn't even eaten yet.

"So it's really all going to end in catastrophe?" Ilana asked. "Is that the way it has to be?"

She turned on the radio, smooth jazz. "Jan's studying the history of anarchism," she said. "I've given it some thought. And I agree it's tempting. It would be so wonderful. But I just can't bring myself to believe people are actually capable of becoming independent-minded enough to decide for them-selves. Most people want to obey authority. They'd rather keep doing the same thing than try to break their habits. Free man is just an illusion."

"Free man is an ideal," I said. "Either you believe in it or you don't. But maybe the point is just to admit that it isn't always the greediest and the strongest who win, the ones who con-sume and destroy the most. The future actually favors people who can cooperate and build something over the long term. The point is to start thinking about how to make this model work. Can it? Maybe. Nobody yet has proved otherwise."

Marius nodded. "American democracy is the biggest scam of all. Saying you can decide everything for yourself, but the moment you step even just a little out of line, poof, that's it. This system's got about as much compassion as old Ceaușescu had. Just look at the people riding the subway home from work. They don't give a damn. All tuned out with their headphones and earbuds. Blank looks. Running on empty. Get home and turn on the TV. What is that if not totalitarian? The final stage of brainwashing. And then there's China, my friends. We can build whatever we want here, but they're still going to have the last laugh. Maybe they'll keep a few high-minded Westerners, for observation and entertainment's sake, just as proof of our failed experiment."

I left around two in the morning. Marius stayed. Ilana walked me downstairs so she could unlock the front door. When we got to the second floor, I suddenly blurted out that I had left my phone upstairs. I sprinted back up the steps to her apartment. It was hanging there in the entryway. His brown leather jacket. I gathered up my saliva, spit on the sheepskin collar, and quietly closed the door behind me.

Back downstairs, I got a kiss on each cheek and stepped outside into the freezing rain.

I needed to cool off, so I walked the whole way home.

When I got home, I didn't feel like going to bed yet, so I turned on my computer to see what was new. Nothing had changed in the past few days. Protests against state budget cuts were still raging in Europe. People smashing shop windows and burning cars. Hundreds of gallons of oil gushing into the ocean from a broken pipe nobody knew how to fix. Thousands of people dying in a country hit by floods, but it was the third one this year already, so no one really cared. The Chinese had taken a crew of Vietnamese fishermen hostage, and the Japanese had taken a captain in the Chinese navy.

On the Web site of *Democracy Now*, I found an interview by Amy Goodman with Derrick Jensen, the environmental activist Ilana had been talking about earlier.

Jensen, who was born in 1960, says there's no way to prevent the end of civilization.

No way of life based on exploitation can go on forever, he

says. The end is coming soon and we need to prepare for it by actively dismantling civilization. First the cities. And the dams. People have to learn to cook over a fire again and gather edible plants, restore our direct relationship with what we consume.

There's a lot of work ahead of us, for everyone. Let's stop wasting time pretending things can go on the way they are. With fewer and fewer salmon returning to the rivers every year, you don't have to be a genius to figure out that eventually there won't be any left.

The only sustainable way of living, says Jensen, was in the Stone Age, and there's no doubt we'll end up there again; it's just a question of what will be left when we get there. How many animal and plant species will have to go extinct, how many poisons we'll have to put into our systems.

We all have blood on our hands, he says.

He says he learned about violence and the dynamics of power from his father, who abused him.

It occured to me that the first generation of anarchists, the radical prophets of human freedom, were also raised by abusive fathers and teachers. Their rebellion against God and the state was the rebellion of sons and daughters against their fathers.

It must have been all the wine I drank. As I lay in bed, sinking into sleep, I suddenly felt dizzy. I saw myself from on high, just a tiny person stuck on the massive body of planet Earth, hurtling through the dark reaches of space at 67,000 miles per hour. As the ice and rubble whizzed past my ears, in my mind I hear the end of a poem Ilana recited to me once, back in the fall: "Do you hear the bullet flying over our heads? Do you hear the bullet waiting—for our kiss?"

THE NEXT DAY, IN THE MIDDLE OF WINTER, suddenly spring explodes.

It's so warm when I go out for a walk in Central Park that evening, I even unbutton my coat. By the pump house on the reservoir, sitting on a bench that got enough sun during the day to dry out, is an elderly woman with curly black hair and a dark-colored poncho. I see her there often.

She always sits in the same spot. She usually has a paper sack on her lap, and when nobody is looking, she throws a handful of food behind the bench to a group of raccoons.

I talked to her once. She said she looks after the raccoons, which the city is threatening to exterminate because there are too many of them in the park and they have rabies.

"Instead of taking care of them," she said, "they want to kill them." She knew all there was to know about the life of urban raccoons, and when we said good-bye, she handed me a business card: MADAM ESPOSITO, FORTUNE-TELLING, PALM READING, TAROT.

"If you ever need anything, give me a call," she said. "Or just stop by."

Today, instead of food, all she has on her lap is a ball of colored yarn. A pair of knitting needles flashes in her fingers— white and swollen, with red-painted nails—clinking against her rings. She looks up and smiles.

"Nothing for your friends today?" I ask.

She gives me a wink and lifts a portion of the sweater she's knitting to reveal the sack of food underneath.

"Too early," says Madam Esposito. "Raccoons don't come out till after sunset."

A chill rises off the surface of the water, but it's quite cozy here behind the pump house.

"Can I join you for a while?"

"Want me to read your palm, huh? Normally, I charge twenty, but I'll give you a discount.

"Left," she commands. She gathers up the knitting and the bag of food from her lap and takes my hand in hers. She squeezes and probes it, viewing it from different angles, bringing it closer to her eyes, then moving it away, the way far-sighted people do when they're trying to focus on something.

"So, what do you want to know?" Madam Esposito asks. "Love, money, health? You don't have money and never will, but you'll manage somehow. I see a pen. Do you write? Health looks good. I see something showing up after forty, but nothing serious. No operations. A few women. One of them could be for you. But there's a barrier between you that'll be hard to overcome. You see that star and cross here? That means it's time for you to start."

"Start what?"

She gives my hand a squeeze in her soft, warm palms. "Grabbing hold of life and squeezing it for all it's worth. But that woman I mentioned," Madam Esposito goes on, "you might want to break up with her. She's not really available and never will be. You'd have to adapt to her. Which would work, but it'd be a struggle and you'd end up losing a lot. She isn't here to have fun. She's what you call a femme fatale. See that mask? That's her. A woman like that just goes her own way and takes you along for the ride. She's stronger than you, even if she may not look it.

"Break up with her," she says.

There's a rustling behind the bench. Madam Esposito strokes my hand, then lets it go.

"Just give me ten if you have it," she says.

She carefully folds the ten-dollar bill into a square and slips it beneath the folds of her poncho. "Thanks. Now go. You'll just scare them off. Raccoons aren't used to company, the little sweeties."

13

THINK PEOPLE SHOULD GET TO KNOW NEW YORK in their twenties, not when they're pushing forty.

I can't muster the same excitement I felt my first time here. The bustling, humming crowds that once so enchanted me now seem like just a mob of lonely neurotics. With their cell phones, iPads, iPods, e-readers, and headphones, the vacant expressions that can transform in a split second into a grimace of sheer terror. Like the time I was crossing the street and a woman in front of me suddenly started backing up. She ran into my shoulder and screamed as if I'd punched her in the stomach: "Wha—Wha—What's going on?"

"Why are you backing up?"

The woman was bent over forward, fending off something invisible with both hands, gasping for breath.

"Can I help you?"

She looked at me in horror, as if I were actually threatening her. I didn't know what else to do except walk away.

Which had changed more? The city or me?

I'm thirty-nine. Just a few years older than Andrei was when Louise went to meet him at the train station in Chicago (she refused to go to Pittsburgh). The "girlfriend" he would never want again.

Louise wrote of that day:

*I wait on the platform alone, apart from the others. I don't
want the comrades to see what's going on inside me. I hide my
face behind the bouquet, nibbling at the rose petals in nervous-
ness. They taste bitter.*

*Fourteen years ago, he left me a young man, full of life. The
man walking toward me along the platform now is bent and
frail, leaning on his cane, squinting into the sunlight from
behind thick lenses.*

*Two months ago, after thirteen and a half years, I was finally
allowed to visit Andrei in prison. I pretended I was his sister. I
spoke to him in Russian and got away with it, although I suspect
they recognized me. My face is in the papers too much to have
fooled them.*

*He didn't speak a word the whole hour, didn't even look me
in the face. He just sat with his head bowed, holding my hand,
weeping and playing with the pendant on my watch.*

Had he gone mad?

*Afterward, he wrote me a letter explaining that he had been
too overcome by his feelings to speak. So instead he focused
on my pendant, a shiny trinket that for him embodied all his
dreams of freedom, all his desire built up over the course of those
thirteen and a half years.*

*In prison he had seemed more powerful. Out here, in the
open air, in this space, he seems shrunken and shriveled. All
those strong, healthy people rushing past him with no inkling
that their faces are like a revelation to him. This simple walk
down the platform, the steps they are taking with no pleasure,*

even with a sense of fatigue, for a long time had been nothing but a painful dream to him.

Silently, we hug. Words cannot bridge a gap of fourteen years. We will have to wait until time catches up to us, until we can settle into the present together again.

Andrei wrote:

She was waiting for me on the platform, her face hidden behind a bouquet of red roses. We hugged and exchanged a few awkward words.

I had to endure a few public appearances, first in Chicago, then in New York. Crowds of people came, celebrating me like a hero. None of it made any sense. My throat tightened up, I was shaking. All I wanted was to be back in my cell. After I fainted at one rally and had to be carried offstage, Louise finally took me home.

But what a home it was!

Louise had changed. She had turned into a loud, confident woman who took charge of her surroundings and didn't brook the slightest sign of disagreement. During the time I was in prison, she had had several lovers, including perhaps some women. She nearly married once. All of this she admitted to me quite openly, and yet she expected us to pick up where we had left off.

When I left, she was still a girl. Now she was a mother, only without children. Her apartment in Harlem, which also served as storage space and the magazine's offices, was an open-door salon, friends and friends of friends turning up unannounced at all hours of the day and night to debate, smoke, drink coffee, and wine if there was any. Louise, if she had time, cooked meals for everyone.

But I needed peace! Peace and quiet, a small, enclosed space that I could slowly, gingerly crawl my way out of, feeling my way through the terrain, so different from what I had imagined while I was in prison. I needed someone I could tell about my life in Allegheny. About the months of cold, wet solitude and darkness, about how I squatted in a heap of my own excrement and nearly went blind from the beatings.

Instead, I found myself in Louise's apartment. Everyone asked how I felt, but they never waited to hear my response. They walked around me like I was a piece of old family furniture. No use for it, but we can't throw it away. What do we do with it?

I slept with Louise's secretary, but that didn't help. I dreamed of prison every night. I wanted to go back. The world outside made no sense.

Then one day, Louise took me out of town. She borrowed a house from her friends in the hills on the Hudson. Instead of going on lecture tours, she stayed at home and cooked for me. She wanted to be physically intimate again. She criticized the habits I had developed in prison and now so fearfully clung to. She begged me to go back to being the old Andrei she knew.

We had different opinions on many things. Louise couldn't forgive me for refusing to praise Czolgosz's assassination of McKinley. She stood up for the Polish-American radical against those who claimed that his act had doomed the anarchist movement in America. Hadn't they said the same thing about me fourteen years ago? How could I defend my own actions while saying the assassination of the president was pointless? Not even fourteen years in prison gave me the right to elevate myself over anyone else.

I tried to explain (as I had in the letter to her I had smuggled out of prison immediately after the assassination, the letter she said had "so wounded her") that our goal wasn't simply to blindly carry out ideas. The precision of an assassination was what gave it value. Derived from a precise assessment of the situation.

If I had succeeded in killing Kolman fourteen years ago, it might actually have changed something. There was nobody who could have replaced him. Kolman's power stood or fell with him and him alone. Nobody else would have called in the army. Whoever took his place would probably have negotiated with the workers. The unions might have won a victory, serving as an example and an encouragement to other, similar attempts. In the end, who knows? America might actually have swung over to our side.

But what was gained by the death of a president? Nothing at all. He was just a puppet of the capitalists; his power was purely abstract. McKinley could be replaced, as we saw after the assassination. Not to mention he was popular, a fact that now works against us.

MENTALLY, ANDREI DIDN'T COME HOME from prison until he felt he was needed. During the government's nationwide campaign against anarchists, the police in California planted a bomb and pinned it on two of his comrades. Andrei took up their defense, writing articles, delivering speeches, collecting signatures and money. Eventually, he moved to San Francisco and started his own magazine. He took Louise's secretary with him, but that was the least of the blows as far as she was concerned.

14

LANA SPENT THE NIGHT AT MY PLACE and told me about the day she had stopped loving her husband.

She remembered clearly the morning she realized it was over.

A young woman was walking down their street, pulling a defiant child by the hand and leading a dog on a leash. The dog was rust-colored. The woman had a green beret pulled down over her head, a brown sweater tightly hugging her soft, bulging belly and hips. Her round-tipped lace-up boots ground against the small stones of white-and-blue-gray granite strewn with yellowing sycamore leaves. The woman turned and gave an inquisitive glance back at the silver car parked by the curb, where Ilana sat inside, hands primly folded in her lap, looking straight ahead. In the bright blue sky, high above, a ray of sun flashed off a pigeon's belly.

She told her husband she didn't want to live with him anymore. There was an emptiness at the center of her life he couldn't fill.

Keeping quiet isn't the same as silence. Silence is negative, the imprint of a scorched body, a black shadow on the wall. Shadows rolling over one another, dips and trenches, currents that drag her down and sweep her away. But there are places to rest, quiet glades, clearings amid the noisy underbrush, where things stabilize, even if just for a moment or two.

She didn't know how to act once it was actually over. She had never thought about what would happen when love came to an end. For years it had been there, a warm and glowing core. Like the black dot with the edge of flame that flared up before her eyes if she stared into a candle for long enough.

The fact that her love for her husband could come to an end undermined her trust in everything else.

She could end her own life, too.

Or take antidepressants, like some of her friends, and go for a fuck in Timişoara every now and then.

"Why should we break up?" her husband asked. "Do whatever you want—just don't tell me about it." That was his suggestion, and he followed it. Perhaps he already had for some time.

She could see herself clearly: full of destructive, aimless desire. Men didn't understand what was going on, but they followed her around clumsily. Most of them were cheating on someone, straining against their short leashes.

What did she think of when she heard the word *happiness*? The day she and her boy went out in the park after a winter storm, trampling paths through the fresh-fallen snow and knocking the caps of white from the low-standing lamps lining the sidewalks, when suddenly the chef of the Bellevue came running out of his restaurant. He skipped down the icy steps, only his white coat and apron on, and as he passed, he stopped a moment and lifted the boy into the air. The slopes of the surrounding hills loomed blue, the tiny lights of windows and lanterns sparkling in the distance.

There was happiness in her daily routine, the tangible details, the smells, the regular routes she traveled together with her child that embedded themselves in her heart, as if home were all the places the two of them had spent their time, day in day out, those first months and years. She missed them. The pond her boy threw rocks into for what seemed like forever, the frozen road she tramped along, her own impatience and boredom.

She had been as dependent on her husband as a child. Their love had been the starting point from which everything else unfolded.

One day, she woke up in the middle of the night and looked herself in the face. It was the face of death, dressed in festive summer clothes. Her own death smiling stiffly back at her.

She has dreams of New York City submerged underwater. The streets silent, not a soul around. She thinks of the icebergs, slowly melting as they drift away from the poles. The elusive images rapidly crumbling away.

She wishes she had her child with her.

Ilana fell silent. I didn't know what to say, and I was afraid to take her in my arms. She lay next to me on the bed, fully clothed, hands pressed to her face.

Pain translated into words tends to come across as banal. I suppose it's the same with happiness, except you aren't so alone with it.

She didn't move. Outside, a lone window shone through a crack in the paper blinds, so high up in the dark that it looked suspended in the sky.

"IF I WENT ON A TRIP," Josef asked me one day, "would you take care of my papers?"

"Where do you want to go?"

"I don't know yet." He shrugged. "I was just wondering."

He talked about his "trip" fairly often after that. I didn't suspect a thing, I swear. Josef was my best friend. He may have looked like a downer, but he was actually a lot of fun. He always had been, ever since he was a kid.

Then one day, he started saying he was going to stop writing.

"Sad things are all I can write about," he said, "and the world already has more than enough of that. Why add to it? It should be just the opposite. I should try to fill people with optimism and hope, instead of pointing out the meaninglessness that everyone goes through every day. It's perverse, don't you think? Books should either be enjoyable or enlightening. But I can't write books like that."

That was just before he had his first success. One of his novels was translated into German and got excellent reviews. Josef bought a new sport coat and traveled abroad a few times. But it did nothing to change his views. As far as he was concerned, the fact that people enjoyed his gloomy, plodding prose was just proof that they were afflicted with the same perversion that drove him to write.

"It's like a disease," he told me.

Over the years I got used to the fact that he lived alone. I knew he'd made a few attempts to find someone, all of which were a fiasco. Living in a small town, his choice was limited. But he didn't complain, and eventually I started wondering if he might be gay and not realize it. I had all kinds of theories.

The conversation I played in my head word by word while Ilana pretended to be asleep was from my last visit to L.

Josef made potato soup and I brought the wine. Everything

was as usual, except that he seemed anxious and excited at the same time. Like he was gearing up for something.

Other times we would talk about everything under the sun, jumping from gossip and trivial insights one minute to earth-shaking ideas the next. Each of us had a good memory, and whenever we could, we would pick up from where we'd left off the last time we got together. We even had quite a few laughs. But not this time.

Josef said he had something he wanted to confide in me. He was smiling.

As usual, Josef's smile seemed out of place. His eyes, nose, and mouth were crowded into the middle of his widespread face, as if driven there with a whip. It was a face that gave the impression of violence and an intense inner life, almost touching in its ugliness. The smile didn't belong there.

"Go ahead."

"It can wait."

Finally, after midnight, the time came. I was tired, a little drunk, and incapable of any serious reflection. That was probably what he was waiting for. Maybe he was too shy to confide in me while I still had all my senses. He didn't want my advice or opinion; he just needed me to hear him out, patiently—even numbly.

He said that for several years now he had been in love with a woman. She was married and from L., but he couldn't reveal who she was. He wanted to live with her, but she didn't feel the same.

"I know she loves me," Josef said. "But she's afraid of me. She says I'm odd. She doesn't know what to think of my writing and she finds me depressing."

"She said that?"

"Basically, yes."

The woman he had loved for several years now, Josef went on, was pregnant. He found out about it by accident—she didn't even tell him herself. She wanted to give the baby up. She didn't want to get divorced and she didn't think Josef would make a very good father.

"Does she already have any kids?"

"No."

"Then how come?"

"It's my fault," said Josef. "I'm just not good enough for her."

As if the bar weren't set high enough already. As if we couldn't just crawl under it in the end, and why not! Who would judge us for it? I got angry. At that stupid woman, but also at Josef. I was disappointed in him. I didn't expect such a banal secret coming from him.

"Is there any way I can help?" I asked.

"I don't think so," he said. "At first I thought you might be able to talk to her. But now I have the feeling it wouldn't be a good idea."

I agreed.

About a month later, I got a call from him out of the blue saying that he was in Prague and asking if we could get together. I told him I had to go out of town on a work trip for the day but that I might make it back in time to meet if I could get a lift. I gave him the name of a café and said if I didn't show up by ten, that meant I couldn't make it. I found out afterward he had waited for me till closing time. Three days later, he was dead.

What did he mean, anyway, when he asked me to take care of his papers? Was I supposed to find a publisher for them? Destroy them? Donate them to the National Archives? There were no instructions in his good-bye letter. He just apologized to his sister for the trouble his death would cause her, then added, "Please give all my papers to Jan. He'll know what to do."

Josef's death weighed on me. I had to do something. Feeling sorry wouldn't help anyone, and it was too late to give my friend a hug, but if nothing else I could pick up his project where he had left off. I felt like I owed it to him. I would continue his research on Andrei B. and write the book I had found a fragment of in the notebook with the blue cover.

It made no difference if Andrei B. was my great-grandfather or not. Professor Kurzweil was right.

The crack between the drawn blinds was starting to fill with light when Ilana snuggled up to me. We hugged each other like shipwreck survivors, my face buried in her shoulder. I knew this time she was mine for real. Open and dangerously close. I couldn't be tender. I was too afraid. I entered her as if I were pushing her away.

15

THE SUN SETS BEHIND THE TOWERS of the old apartments on the west side of the reservoir. To the northeast, the moon hangs, a thin strip of pale light tacked onto a sweep of dark blue. The first star. As the darkness reaches under the bushes, smells rise to my nostrils, unwinding with the easing of the summer heat.

The runners chat as they make their way around the reservoir, the women's high voices carrying across the surface. Some wave their arms like wings; some bob side to side. Some run stiff-legged. Some snort loudly, spraying sweat. A runner with perfect form flashes past. I can't tell whether man or woman; the narrow hips and slender limbs could just as well be either. They run with a light step, lifting their knees high, hair fluttering despite the lack of wind. They hold their crossed arms tightly to their chest, head tipped slightly back, eyes half-closed.

I walk over to the pump house on the dike. On the bench, out of reach of the lanterns' orange glow, I can just make out the generous silhouette of Madam Esposito. I wave hello and walk toward her quietly, so as not to scare away any raccoons.

"How are you doing?"

"Good, thanks," says the psychic. "And you?"

"I'm good, too. Lovely evening, isn't it?"

"Beautiful."

I open and quickly close my hand, as if I'd caught an insect. She smiles.

"See you tomorrow, then," I say.

"Yes, see you then."

ILANA AND I ARE "FRIENDS" NOW. It happens to me more often than I'd like. As soon as a woman starts to confide too much in me, I know how it's going to end. As far she's concerned, I'm no longer a potential partner, but more like a friend or brother.

I think she's going out with Marius. His scholarship at the arts center on the Hudson ran out, but he moved to New York to be near her.

Professor Kurzweil practically hasn't left his house since winter. I go see him twice a week. I don't understand how he can be so isolated after spending more than seventy years in the same city.

We talk about all kinds of things, including suicide. The professor says he can easily imagine it. We talk about how Andrei B. ended his life and I tell him about Josef.

God played no role in the life of either man. They weren't interested in any notion of a higher power. They based their decisions solely on their assessment of the situation here in the world of physical laws, of cause and effect. Professor Kurzweil says he believes the true cause of Josef's suicide wasn't his struggles with love, but the extreme need for inner purity, which he was probably born with. And which is a greater hindrance to normal life than any physical defect.

"I don't believe in God, either," he says. "Not that I'm

so brave. I dabbled in it a fair amount myself, before I met Erica. It's almost impossible to face that emptiness alone, and I was alone. Completely alone, except for an uncle who came to America back in the early thirties. My parents, grandparents, younger siblings, they all died in the war. Though I'm not sure family can really protect you, either. Maybe they just soften the blows a little. You can be rescued only by someone who attaches himself to you by choice. That bond between two unrelated people," he said, "is a miracle. I didn't take into account the fact that Erica was mortal. I always thought she would outlive me."

We listen to music together. The professor loves Janáček and Mahler. He guided me through all of Mahler's symphonies, up until the unfinished Tenth, which he doesn't like.

He said he used to like to listen to it when he was younger. He was fascinated by the final, interrupted tone. But it wasn't exciting to him anymore. In fact, nothing was more familiar to him, more real, than the broken note, the word he would one day, maybe tomorrow, fail to finish saying, writing, hearing.

He stopped the record and pointed out its unique lack of unity, the fragmentary nature of Mahler's music, how it seems to be constantly falling apart, the motifs butting heads with one another, fighting to be heard, a heroic struggle for unity that now, however, belongs to the past, since even the best experiments perish in a vacuum. That was the beginning of the twentieth century, Europe before World War I. From Mahler on, no one would be able to think or write coherently. "Do you hear the fragments of all those beautiful melodies, forever lost to everyone who comes after Mahler?

"And yet," he continued, "ultimately Mahler always finds

the way to redemption. After all the struggles and empty promises, his music is saved by something extremely tender and intimate. A single note or a quiet human voice."

I'll be going back to Prague soon. My friends send e-mails, asking if I'm looking forward to coming home and what I got out of my stay. Did I write the book I was talking about? Did I at least start it?

I reply that I'm still in the research phase. Josef's notebook has gotten a lot thicker since I've been in New York, but it isn't clear how all the parts fit into a whole.

Professor Kurzweil is right. What's the use in pretending there's unity where there isn't any? Why make things up? Why not let the individual fates rub up against one another as randomly as the sheets of paper stuck into the blue notebook?

John C. Kolman and Andrei B.

My great-grandmother Friederike and Eleanor C. Kolman.

Professor Kurzweil and I. And Ilana.

On my last visit, the professor announced that he was selling his gorgeous apartment on the west side of Central Park and moving to a retirement home outside the city.

Eleanor C. Kolman died. Sister Michaela wrote to let me know, saying she thought it might interest me. She had stopped eating and passed away in the early spring.

The letter from Sister Michaela sounded mystical.

She wrote that the night her great-aunt died, she suddenly woke up and couldn't get back to sleep. She got dressed and quietly crept outside, so as not to wake the other nuns. It was cool and so bright that she could see the puffs of air coming out of her mouth condensing in little clouds. She walked through the garden, across the lawn, and down the driveway to the gate, passing the building that was going to be the new canteen. From the north, the convent was shielded by a concrete wall about two meters high; from the south, there was just a fence of wooden planks with narrow cracks revealing glimpses of the sky. The wind whistled through the cracks, carrying grains of orange sand and dust. The gate in the middle of the wall was locked, but Michaela, as one of the older sisters in charge, had a key. To her right towered the rough-hewn edifice of the church, its concrete walls shining eerily, and past them, the peaks of St. Peter's, still white with snow.

She left behind the convent and the church, walking along the dirt road through the sagebrush and cactus plants.

The landscape around her was taut with silence as it slipped into the gap between night and day. The animals of the night crawled back into their holes, clearing the way for the dead. This time belonged to them.

She heard the sound of her own footsteps, the creak of tiny pebbles under her soles, the rustle of her habit's heavy fabric. She knew she was not alone; her great-aunt was walking with her.

A wind kicked up and the eastern sky turned gray. A morning bird called out from an acacia bush.

She turned to make her way back. By now she could clearly make out the woods on the mountainside, the crest of peaks, rising and falling through a cover of clouds. The mountain has its own rainfall, Michaela wrote to me. It fills the streams that spring from its sides, feeding thousands of rare species of herbs, trees, and animals.

Twice a week, the sisters drive to one of the springs in a pickup truck, its bed full of plastic barrels. They use the water to make the dough for communion wafers, which they supply to half of the eighty parishes and missions in the diocese of Tucson. They bake every day except Sundays and holidays. They have machines for mixing and kneading, but the rolling out and everything else they do by hand.

Sister Michaela also wrote that although she had been a disappointment to her great-aunt, Eleanor had left her a lot of money. She said she was donating part of it to the convent, but most of it she planned to divide between a few select charities. She didn't want to set up her own foundation, since she didn't want her gift associated with the name of her great-grandfather Kolman. She wanted the money dispersed with as little attention as possible.

16

I WOULDN'T HAVE BELIEVED IT POSSIBLE in a city of twelve million people. I ran into them in Brooklyn, in a neighborhood where none of us lives. All of a sudden, they came out of a side street in front of me, just walking along holding hands. Ilana slightly taller than Marius, slender, in a summery red T-shirt and bright-colored shorts, hair pinned to her scalp in an improvised bun leaning precariously to one side.

I caught up with them at the intersection, where they had stopped to wait for the light. There was no way to pretend I hadn't seen them.

"Well, well, well, if it isn't our anarchist." Marius smiled. He was always that obnoxious; I'd gotten used to it by now. Ilana didn't seem bothered. "What are you doing here?"

"I was at a gallery. What about you?"

"Oh, just taking a walk around." He laughed, as if he'd said something witty.

"We're going to see some friends," said Ilana. "Want to come?"

"Why wouldn't he?" Marius said, turning to her. "At least he'll meet some other people."

I shrugged. "Why not?"

We stopped in front of an old house made of brick. Marius reached through the bars on the gate and opened the latch from inside. We stepped up to the green-painted front door and rang the bell.

A short blond girl came to answer, between twenty and twenty-five, I'd say. She gave Marius and Ilana a kiss on both cheeks, then greeted me the same way.

"I'm Mia."

"This is Jan," Ilana introduced me before I could do it myself. "He's writing a book on anarchism."

"For real?"

"I'm a historian," I said.

"Oh." She sounded disappointed. "Come on in."

We walked down a dark, narrow hallway and out an open door into a shaded backyard, where most of the guests were gathered. Maybe twenty people in all. I was clearly the oldest.

Young men and women sat smoking hand-rolled cigarettes, drinking beer and tea. They helped themselves to the latter from a large pot resting on one of the concrete steps. Mia, acting as hostess, asked what we wanted to drink. She said there was beer in the kitchen fridge if we wanted, and if we'd brought anything, we could put it in there.

I blushed, but luckily Marius pulled two six-packs of bottled beer from his knapsack and padded off into the house with them.

Ilana looked around. "Is he here yet?"

"Not yet," said Mia. "But he called to say he was sorry for being late."

The backyard conversation moved along at a low hum, every now and then one of the guests looking up toward the door, as if expecting someone. It reminded me of the atmosphere under communism in Prague, back in the eighties, when I was in high school and we would go to illegal seminars taught by professors in people's apartments.

"Is someone special coming?" I asked Ilana in a hushed voice.

"Yeah," she said. "An amazing guy. I'm really glad you're going to meet him. Actually I don't know why I didn't invite you in the first place. I should have called you. He's a true revelation, in my opinion."

"What does he do?"

"He's a philosopher," Marius answered for her, emerging from behind us with three chilled bottles of Brooklyn Lager. "My new guru." He laughed.

"So no more Žižek?"

He laughed again. "Žižek? He's obsolete. I'm tired of the same old right-left rhetoric. Nobody would do anything if it were up to him. He's all talk and no action."

We sat down on a concrete step warmed by the sun, sipping our beers as we eavesdropped on the conversations around us.

"Capitalism's got another fifty years, max. The accumulation of capital can't go on forever. There are physical limits, and sooner or later it's going to run up against them."

"The question is, What comes after?"

"It might be even worse."

"Personally," said a hardy-looking young man with a blond beard and a ruddy face, "I don't plan on being around for it. Whenever I have any free time, I take off for the mountains. My brother and I head up there and practice survival techniques. Plus, I also signed up for a gardening course."

"That's great," said a girl with a pageboy cut and a silver

stone in her nose. "But instead of preparing ourselves for the worst, shouldn't we be thinking about how to keep it from coming to that?"

"I just want to be ready."

"We should all be ready."

"He's here," Ilana said, jabbing me in the side.

I'm going to call him Daniel. Tall, skinny, arms covered with a light layer of blond hair and dotted with freckles sticking out of his short-sleeved plaid summer shirt. Close-cropped blond hair, thinning on top. Silver-framed glasses. Straight, narrow face. Strong chin. Maybe a little bit older than I was, somewhere between forty and fifty. Maybe closer to fifty. Wearing a little backpack. Standing next to him, a short, heavyset woman with a mop of rust-colored curls. They looked like a pair of English tourists.

Everyone lined up to shake his hand, one by one.

They arranged their chairs in a circle. Daniel accepted an open bottle of beer from Mia, took a sip, set it down on the ground, and started digging through his backpack, trying to find something. The bottle fell over and he blushed, flashing an apologetic grin.

"Daniel," said Mia, and I suddenly realized how genuinely kind she was. "We're so glad you could be with us today."

Everyone smiled and nodded their heads. Daniel visibly relaxed.

"Maybe," he said, putting his papers away in his backpack, "we could start with some questions."

"Should we raise our hands?" asked an Indian-looking young man with long hair.

"That would be better," said Mia.

His hand shot up in the air. All I understood of his question was that it had something to do with personal identity. He talked a long time, stuttering and saying the word *like* repeatedly.

Everyone there except me knew something about Daniel's theory already, so he didn't bother rehashing the basics. I was a little bit lost.

If I understood correctly, Daniel was arguing that personal identity as such doesn't exist. The only thing that remains constant about an individual over time is a certain degree of continuity in thinking and our connection to a network of external relations.

"We fear the future because it's *our* future," said Daniel, "but by the time we reach that point, which we can only guess at today, it won't be us anymore. All that we'll have in common with the person we are today is a few memories, some reference points, some of the content of our thoughts, but nothing any deeper. The world doesn't stand or fall with us. It was here before we came, and will be here long after we're gone. The network exists independent of our physical existence, and we will remain plugged into it, in some form or other, even after we die. A form of immortality, if you will."

Nothing deeper exists beyond the loose bundle of perceptions, needs, desires, and alliances that we call the self, said Daniel. No core, no mystical center, no mysterious homogeneous entity. Once we realize that this assumption about our identity—as something that needs to be protected and in whose interest we need to act—is false, we'll automatically start to care more for our surroundings. Not only for humans, but also for animals, plants, microorganisms, the whole incredibly complex tissue that binds it all together, from the tiniest level all the way up to the largest, everything we can positively confirm.

Abandoning this false notion of the subject means abandoning the theory that everything we do, we do for our own benefit. It means admitting we are capable of sacrifice and self-denial for the benefit of the whole. Putting real issues before self-serving ones, life before death.

"You ask, what really matters? What can I do? Reduce or eliminate suffering by any means possible. Lift the floodgates. Allow the sap to flow freely into every part of the organism. As living beings, we are part of a universal experiment. Our consciousness cannot be separated from it, nor can it fully reflect it. Compassion begins where knowledge ends. Everything else is hubris, including the concept of God."

Daniel might sound like a Buddhist, but he's not, Marius explained on the way back to Manhattan. Though there were some points of overlap. Daniel had written two books so far; each one had taken him ten years. He proved his conclusions through a series of strictly logical steps. Originally, he was a mathematician.

Rather than sidestepping the economic and political structure that all the other contemporary thinkers exhaust themselves trying to analyze, his theory simply left it out altogether. Other philosophers were too married to their hierarchical vision of society, with its concepts of authority, center, and power.

Daniel, explained Marius, described an order of relations

that was inherently democratic. You could even say anarchic, but not in the sense of chaotic.

"In January you were still preaching the dictatorship of the proletariat," I said, needling him.

"Ha-ha," Marius snorted. "You can think what you want, but we mean it!"

"What about you?" I asked Ilana. She had been walking along beside us without saying a word. She glanced up with a puzzled look on her face. She wasn't even listening. Apparently, she couldn't have cared less about the problems of global capitalism.

I touched her arm.

I wished I could make love to her. Slowly and gently, in some quiet, deserted place.

BEFORE I LEAVE FOR PRAGUE, I go to visit Professor Kurzweil one last time. He's in a nursing home now, in a little town on the Hudson.

The train ride along the river, its surface dotted with drizzling rain, reminds me of my Halloween weekend with Ilana. It was a beautiful, clear morning and Ilana was taking pictures from the train. She had a manual camera that shot film, the kind nobody used anymore. She told me she loved the click of the body snapping shut when she loaded a roll of film. The whir of the spool as she advanced to the next frame. She liked setting the aperture and shutter speed, the smell of the camera's leather case. She saved all her prints with the bent corners, along with her paper letters and postcards, ticket stubs from galleries and concerts, punched train tickets. She couldn't throw any of it away. Evidence that she had actually lived.

The rain keeps coming down, the gray curtain of water and mist shrouding the view of the opposite bank. I take a cab from the train station.

The retirement home looks like a hotel, except for the handrails and buzzers installed all over the place. The hallways smell like a hospital. The professor invites me into his room. It has a kitchenette and everything is bright and clean, if a little bit cramped. I recognize a few pieces of furniture from his old apartment in Manhattan, as well as part of his library, but most of his things he had to get rid of.

I praise the beautiful view from the window, the fresh air and nature so close by.

He shrugs. "I would have preferred a café, believe me. Smoke-filled, as it should be."

He says it was hard getting used to the new environment, but he hasn't let it get him down. There are a few people here he can talk to about history or psychoanalysis. They also listen to music together. On days when he feels up to it, he tries to work on his memoirs. A sure sign of vanity, but it isn't as if he is forcing anyone to read it. He just wants to get it all straight in his mind. His own memory surprises him sometimes. All kinds of details come back to him when he is writing—colors, smells. As a matter of fact, when they called him from the reception desk to come and get me, he had been in a village in the Pyrenees, on the run from Hitler. It was the month of May and he was fourteen years old.

"The truth is," he says, "I never did get used to living here. Maybe if I had had children."

"Why didn't you go back to Europe, then?"

"Where would I have gone?" He smiles. "Erica was American, her family was here. I could have left after she died, but it isn't my home anymore. There's nobody there alive, no one who would remember. Unless I count the walls, the cobblestones, a tree or two."

He pauses a moment, then mutters, "Maybe they do count."

After another moment or two, he says, "So what about you? Did you get to the bottom of your famous family tie?"

"No," I say, "but that wasn't the point anyway. It was just an excuse."

"An excuse? For what?"

He doesn't understand, and for it to make any sense, I'd have to go all the way back to twenty years ago, when I said good-bye to him and his wife in the entryway of their New York apartment. I'd have to tell him about Josef. About the debt I feel toward him. Love may weaken over time, but not guilt. Guilt is stronger than death.

The rain has stopped, so I decide to go back to the station on foot. The professor accompanies me as far as the front gate and stands, leaning on his walker, watching as I walk off down the road, which twists and turns as it descends toward the river. As steam rises off the trees, the valley fills with a hazy light. I realize that was probably the last time I'll ever see Professor Kurzweil alive.

— II —

Josef's
Notebook

1

"THE HAPPIEST DAY OF MY LIFE," Andrei B. wrote in his diary.

When he stepped across the border, he knelt down and pressed his lips to the ground. The fresh, chill scent of the snow reminded him of childhood; his mother's fur collar, damp with her breath.

The deported anarchists stepped onto Soviet soil from Finland on the morning of January 20, 1920. If the group looked wretched after their month spent in the ship's damp hold on the rough winter seas, the welcoming committee the Soviets sent to greet them looked even worse: eyes sunken with fatigue, skin yellowed and drawn tight over their skulls; the women pale, severe, and dressed in black, like nuns.

For the first time since he had shot Kolman, Andrei felt that he existed in the here and now: at this intersection of space and time. The present is monumental, like a newborn infant. Screaming, overflowing with life, everything still yet to come, a lifetime of possibilities just waiting to be revealed.

(A year and a half later, when they were comparing their diaries in Berlin, Louise commented to Andrei, "That's odd. You almost never mention me. As if you were there in Russia all by yourself, and meanwhile, look, I write about you on almost every page: how you were sick, how we got separated in Moscow. . . .")

WHAT WAS WRONG WITH RUSSIA? Which characteristics best described the catastrophe?

The contrast between the desertedness of depopulated cities and the crowds constantly surging and churning, as if fleeing an avalanche. People storming trains, squeezing on, glued to windows, stairs, roofs. For every man knocked off by a tunnel, three more clambered on to take his place. Sometimes they had to shoot the passengers off in bunches to allow the railroad cars to move.

People rush about, banging into one another. Busy, one would think, but in reality wandering lost because the familiar landmarks are gone. The ground torn from under people's feet, nationwide, in a bold experiment. So that no one feels at home, safe; there is nothing to rely on. The traces of former life must be erased and reshuffled every day, and an apparatus has been created for that purpose, the central entity holding and exercising power. Its original purpose has been forgotten; the fervor is all that remains.

The subjects of the apparatus are driven to exhaustion, the demands ever changing, with no discernible logic. The only way to elude its clutches, perhaps, is to stay in motion. Like dancing under the feet of an enraged elephant, or being on a death march. To stop is to die.

The burden, the heavy load. The opposite of baggage. Baggage is something one can (with typical bourgeois flippancy) unload, put down, but with a burden, this isn't an option: Its value is always priceless; its loss, tragic.

So it happens that you return home from an errand and find a stranger in your bed, waving a rubber-stamped paper that proves it belongs to him now. In that moment, the practicality of a cart or a sled that can be loaded with what's left at a moment's notice is fully revealed. In winter, bundles and logs of wood can be dragged by a string.

Worry, worry, worry. The frowning faces of engineers. Short on paper, short on ink, short on prison cells. Organization breaks down on multiple fronts at once, the shortcomings piling up too fast to respond to. Each new solution, in turn, produces a series of new flaws to be addressed, and so on and on. It would be wrong to say the apparatus is not workable; on the contrary, it works hard and happily, but according to its own rules.

Shoes: none available. Bare feet in snow, feet wrapped in rags. Old women in old army boots. High-heeled shoes on the bare feet of young women in Soviet offices.

A little girl with painted lips: "Hey, daddy, looking for company?"

"Hey, daddy, buy some cigarettes? I've got some cigarettes for you, daddy!" Little Nina with big eyes holding ten damp cigarettes in her outstretched hand. She picked them out of the snow after tossing them away a few moments ago when someone said the militia was coming. False alarm.

An older woman standing on the corner of the marketplace, her face pale yet still beautiful, in a long dark coat and scarf. Her nose slim and narrow, with sharply cut nostrils. Clutching in her arms a Japanese vase decorated with green bamboo leaves, her delicate, frost-reddened fingers against the green bamboo leaves.

The quickness with which the woman selling the foulsmelling cabbage soup raises the price when she hears Andrei's accent.

"A crust of bread, daddy, just a little crust. For the love of Jesus Christ!"

WHEN WILL THE REVOLUTION COME to America? Any day now, no? What about Germany and England? Right around the corner, isn't it? Why, that can't be right, comrade. The world revolution will happen any day now, and we'll be saved. Our foreign comrades will come to our rescue.

Moskkommune, Narkomput, Narkominodel. Rations and distribution centers. Commissars and clerks.

"Just sign right here, love. Just one little stroke of the pen, that's all. What harm can it do you? One little stroke!"

A faded, taciturn Kropotkin under house arrest in the countryside.

The Chekists in their black leather coats, naked guns tucked under their belts.

Little Vaska threatening his parents from his bed: "Better watch out or I'll tell on you!" Hunger and fear.

"What time is it?"

"Three under the old system, five under the new. But as of yesterday six, I heard."

Four kinds of rubles: Kerensky, czarist, Ukrainian, Soviet.

In the south, women with dark eyes and olive complexions chew sunflower seeds and spit the hulls on the ground.

Even the prisons aren't what they used to be. You can't read or study there. Not like under the czars. In those days, prison was the best school you could get. Men went in ignorant fools and came out philosophers, theorists. Like Nestor Makhno.

WHEN NESTOR MAKHNO CONQUERS A TOWN, the first thing he does is open up the prison gates. Then he gathers everyone together and gives a speech: "Now organize things your own way."

His young wife, Galina, dashes out onto the street by the morning light in Kharkov: "Why should I be afraid? I'm not afraid. I've always fought alongside Nestor in every battle, and Nestor always fights at the head of his men."

Last year, a woman like her was laughing in the springtime sun on a Moscow park bench.

Up against the wall. Fire.

The quiet of an Easter procession circling St. Isaac's Cathedral. They whisper to one another: "Christ is risen from the dead. But no colored eggs again this year." An emaciated female child rocking side to side in a church alcove to the rhythm of a song that only she can hear.

The bureaucracy of terror, the terror of bureaucracy.

The fanatical bureaucrat Lenin in the Kremlin: "Communism boils down to a matter of proper bookkeeping." The only thing great about him is his loneliness.

Trotsky's message to the Kronstadt sailors: "I'll shoot you like pheasants." Soldiers in white camouflage on the frozen, cracking Neva, soldiers under the ice and dead mutineers in the streets of Kronstadt. Mass executions in the beech groves on the outskirts of Petrograd.

MOSCOW HAS TURNED GREEN AGAIN. Tables with white tablecloths, music streaming from cafés, new shops with freshly painted signs. The New Economic Policy, processions of hunger-deranged ghosts. Big-eyed Nina doesn't sell cigarettes anymore. "Hey, daddy, looking for company?" Crimsoned lips and bare legs. "My mother starved to death. So did little Peter. And Masha."

Some of his American fellow travelers from the *Buford* have joined the Party. He runs into an ex-policeman from Detroit wearing a black leather jacket and carrying a gun. The Chekists get bigger rations, with enough left over to sell. There are other advantages, too.

Andrei doesn't know which way to turn anymore. After receiving a promise that the imprisoned Russian anarchists will be deported to Germany, he looks for a crack through which to escape, together with Louise, who plods through Moscow hunched under a burden of sorrow and disappointment.

Louise takes the Soviet defeat personally, crying on the train to Sweden.

It's a warm, mild September, the birch leaves turning yellow along the route north.

2

"THE TRUTH IS ALWAYS IN MOTION." Andrei isn't sure where he heard this sentence. Maybe from one of the artists who gathered at the Romanische Café, where the revolution was still being planned and the smoke wafted up to the high ceiling and rolled slowly through the rays of afternoon sun.

At the café, Andrei meets the assistant to the pathologist who identified Rosa Luxemburg's body. He confides in everyone that the female corpse with the bullet hole in her head who lay four months at the bottom of the Landwehr Canal was definitely not her, because Rosa had suffered rickets as a child and one of her legs was shorter than the other.

The truth is always in motion.

Sunken eyes—there is hunger in Germany, too—shine through the curtain of smoke. Hunger and tuberculosis, morphine, cocaine. Dilated pupils, flushed cheeks, hands trembling, flitting, quickly, lightly, savoring each breath in and out, the sweet rush of blood. They came to Berlin after spending Christmas in a Stockholm jail. Europe has changed a lot since the war. Wherever they hole up now, they're bound to be viewed with suspicion.

ANDREI HAD JUST TURNED FIFTY and there were days when he felt tired. He started writing a book about Russia, but Louise beat him to it. A publisher in America offered her a contract and an advance. Andrei set aside his work to help Louise edit her book, and offered her his notes. Louise split the advance with him, as she did all the money she got from America.

While Louise struggled with the manuscript, and with a young Swede who had moved in with her, Andrei established a committee for the relief of Soviet political prisoners and their families. He organized funding drives, wrote pleading letters, contacted underground connections to deliver money, food, and clothing to Russia. He felt similar to the way he had when he got out of prison in Pittsburgh after fourteen years. He was free, but his mind was with those who were still behind bars. He was helped with his growing agenda by a volunteer corps of sensitive young women of the sort who always materialize around aging revolutionaries. They were pretty, elegant, smelled wonderfully, and Louise couldn't stand them, because they didn't know the first thing about life, and their sympathy with workers had been sparked by romances with flowery covers gobbled up during the break between lunch and afternoon tea. Fortunately, Andrei didn't last long with any of them. The first one was some girl named Friederike. When she disappeared from the picture, she was replaced by Emma Stein, nicknamed "Mimi."

Naïve and softhearted, Mimi Stein offered Andrei a chance to relax. He hadn't had a home since the age of seventeen, when he left for America, and the longest he had ever stayed in one place was in prison.

Mimi hadn't read Nietzsche or Marx, and was just starting on Kropotkin. She liked him because he was "kind," but she didn't understand his idea of a society based on free association.

All of her experience up to that point suggested the opposite. She believed that some rules were a given and couldn't be created on the spot, anew every time.

On the other hand, she had a strong aversion to violence, oppression, and injustice. She felt terrible whenever she saw poverty and was ready to give away everything she possessed. She was passionate about her work with Andrei and put all her energy into it. She even had a falling-out with her family over it.

"It's so unjust," Louise protested when the young Swede ran off with her secretary after several months of agony. "You'll always have a Mimi around, and meanwhile my blue-eyed Lars is gone. He said I'll be a lifelong inspiration to him. I don't want to be anyone's lifelong inspiration," she complained. "I want someone to love me, to tell me I'm beautiful, even if I'm not! Doesn't Mimi see how old you are? How come she doesn't mind but Lars does? What's the difference between us?"

Andrei silently gave her a hug and Louise burst into tears.

"Even you don't want to be with me!" she wailed. "You didn't want to live with me in Russia, either. And when we were in America, you ran off to San Francisco to get away from me. Don't think I don't realize."

She urged Andrei to apply for a Czechoslovak visa so he could go to Prague. She was leaving soon for England, where friends had been able to make arrangements for her to stay, but not Andrei, and the German authorities were making it more and more difficult for him every day. But Andrei didn't want to go to Czechoslovakia.

He accompanied Louise to the train station. Short, round, and gray-haired, she made her way to the platform and bounded up the stairs onto the train with no need of help. A few moments later, she slammed the compartment window down with a bang. "Whatever you do, don't stay here, or they'll send you back to Russia!" The train pulled out of the station, so he didn't have to come up with a response. He pulled out his handkerchief and waved good-bye, and Louise did the same. He was too far away to see her tears, but he knew she was crying. She had been crying a lot lately.

She's getting old, Andrei thought, even if no one's allowed to say so.

Nestor Makhno, in a donated suit, with a fresh haircut, no horse, and wholly unarmed, sits next to Andrei B. at a round table in the Romanische Café. His wife, Galina, whom he last saw in Kharkov at dawn, is here in Berlin with him. One day Andrei brings Mimi along, and the four of them start getting together regularly.

"The transition to self-rule is entirely natural for agricultural communities," says Makhno. "The problem is the cities, industrial manufacturing. Communist anarchism can only be achieved in the countryside, among the peasant farmers and small craftsmen, where there is a direct relationship between producer, product, and consumer."

Black tea topped up with boiling water, the dense smoke of cigarettes. Mimi brings food for everyone and sits patiently through the debates, which she doesn't understand.

All romance is gone. The disappointment is nearly palpable, and it will be hard for Andrei to rekindle faith in the revolution after what he saw in Russia.

Half the patrons in the café look more romantic than Makhno, the ataman they sang songs and told legends about in Ukraine.

The answer isn't to abandon revolution, but to rethink its theoretical foundations.

Gone are the endless plains and wide-open skies.

After a long series of delays, they obtain a visa to France.

Nestor finds a job in a carpentry shop, while Andrei sits in a cheap rented room, laboring over an introduction to the principles of anarchism, commissioned by a small publisher in the United States. Every month he goes to the local police station to extend his residence permit. For now, Mimi remains in Berlin.

3

LIKE THE REST OF EUROPE, postwar Paris, flooded with Russian émigrés, wasn't too inclined toward anarchists. There was a sharp division between Whites and Reds, and anarchists fell on the Red side of the line.

French officials were more efficient than their Russian counterparts, and also more ruthless. These weren't the capricious, bare-legged women of the Soviet offices, but serious men in suits.

The conscientious clerk protected the state as if it were his own home. It wasn't his job to help beggars who couldn't even speak proper French, but to find out what could be used against them. The moment an immigrant became illegal, the French police would arrest him, put him in handcuffs, and send him over the border on a train with an escort of two armed guards. Because he lacked any valid papers, naturally they didn't want him in Belgium or Switzerland, either, so they sent him back to France, where the authorities locked him up in jail. Upon his release, he got a new deadline to obtain documents, which he of course failed to meet.

Monsieur Jean-Michel Després, for example, a clerk at the police prefecture in Montreuil, had perfected a method for snaring foreigners in a trap that was near escapeproof. By means of bureaucratic procedures, he would maneuver the applicant into a situation where in order to settle his case with

Mssr. Després he required a document that only Mssr. Després was authorized to issue. Thus the two ends of the rope met on Mssr. Després's desk, and it was up to him to determine how tightly to draw the knot.

For a Communist who couldn't even speak proper French and was quite likely a Bolshevik spy, it might not even have been worth going back to France. Instead he could simply disappear and sink into the underground, as so many before him had done. The morally upright Mssr. Després shuddered in horror at the thought of illegality, that innermost circle of hell, leaking its foul stench into the legally consecrated structure of the state. If you didn't have your papers in order, you didn't exist. And no one worked the hidden trapdoor more cunningly than Mssr. Després, the clerk of Montreuil.

This was the same Mssr. Després who every day after lunch took a nap and on Sundays rode the train with his wife and two daughters to the outskirts of Paris, where unfortunately they ran into groups of rowdy and, quite likely, intoxicated foreigners, who didn't even speak proper French and couldn't tell one type of cheese from another. One needed to protect oneself, especially if one had two impressionable daughters.

But one must also know one's enemy. And so it was that Mssr. Després, along with two other gentlemen from the prefecture, daringly, albeit with some reluctance, ventured out into the seamy underbelly of Paris. "Going on expedition," they called it. They drank champagne in nightclubs where half-naked dancers, twisting and grinding, imitated the city's greatest sensation, an American black woman who bared her teeth and hopped around like a monkey, exposing her breasts. Mssr. Després had also seen her in person, and found her performance entertaining, up until the moment that he imagined his daughters onstage in her place.

Under other circumstances, Mssr. Després would have found Andrei B. quite likable. He looked less like a revolutionary than the concerned father of impressionable daughters. The two men were close in age. Andrei spoke quite decent French, and there was a kindly manner about him that led Mssr. Després to confide in him. He, too, was bald, wore thick glasses, and carried a cane. He dressed in a jacket, hat in hand; his unobtrusive manners and deep voice were as befitted a supplicant to the state. True, he was a Jew, but that could be overlooked—under other circumstances.

As things stood now, however, Andrei B. was suspicious on all counts, and even if his looks didn't fit with the menacing sound of the word *anarchist*, Mssr. Després had to take action. It wasn't his place to question the motives of his superiors.

With somewhat of a heavy heart, then, he set his masterful trap, and Andrei fell into it headfirst. He didn't even resist. He politely allowed them to slap on the handcuffs, throw him in jail, and the next day, escorted by two gendarmes, bring him to the Gare du Nord to take the train to Belgium.

4

ANDREI'S MILD GOOD MANNERS had the same effect on the French police whose task it was to escort him over the border and leave him to the mercy of the Belgian authorities as they'd had on Mssr. Després. Over the course of the four-hour journey, they shared their food with him and told him about their families. In return, he described his meeting with Lenin in the Kremlin. They chewed their bread and sausages, marveling at Andrei's report on conditions in Russia. At one point, the younger of them, a man by the name of Jacques Farouche, pounded a fleshy thigh with his fist and said, "It's obvious he's going to end up like Robespierre."

"Who?"

"This Lenin fellow."

"Oh, Robespierre."

The officer softly hummed the old revolutionary ditty: "*Ah! ça ira, ça ira, ça ira! Les aristocrates à la lanterne! Ah! ça ira, ça ira, ça ira! Les aristocrates on les pendra!*"

The traces of the recent war were more visible as they traveled farther north: fields and meadows hemmed in with warning signs, trenches overgrown with grass and deep craters from exploded mines. The crumbled walls of estates that no one would ever return to, rusting tangles of barbed wire. Under a torrent of rain, the flat, fertile land, sloping gradually to sea level in the west, quickly transformed into a sea of mud. Poplar trees and church spires gestured sky-ward. Andrei knew the western front from stories he had heard in New York and Berlin. The men with no legs and no arms had the same look wherever you went, the same bewil-dered silence whenever somebody asked about the war. At the Romanische Café, he had met Otto Dix, one of the few who made it through the war nearly unscathed. He was now recording his memories in a series of graphic prints. Sitting with him silently at his table was a veteran whose lower jaw had been blown off by fragments from a grenade. He sipped his drinks through a straw, holding a napkin in front of the bottom half of his face.

The train came to a stop in the town of Saint-Quentin.

"There was a big ceremony here this year," says Farouche. "The Australian army unveiled a war memorial."

On the platform, they announce the departure of the train to Arras and the older policeman says, "Have you ever heard of the Red Baron?"

"Manfred von Richthofen? They sold postcards of him in Berlin."

"My cousin saw him with his own eyes."

Farouche stretched his face, squinted, and shook his right hand at the wrist. "*Oh là là!*"

THE OLDER POLICEMAN'S COUSIN was named Vincent Grévy. He was twenty-three when the war began. His vision had been poor ever since he was a child, but he enlisted and was assigned to a supply unit on the western front, transporting food and medical supplies. In the spring of 1917, he was in charge of supplies for Britain's Third Army, under General Allenby, who led the Allied attempt to break through German defenses near the French city of Arras.

For months in advance of the attack, the policeman's cousin said, the British engineers oversaw the construction of miles and miles of tunnels in the soft chalk soil underlying the city. The tunnels were dug by Bantam units of miners from northern England and tattooed Maori soldiers from the New Zealand Tunneling Company, who displayed a remarkable talent for laying traps and were able to navigate underground with ease.

They built sleeping quarters for hundreds of soldiers, kitchens, command posts, a hospital, even an underground theater. Some of the corridors had rail tracks running through them, allowing them to move cars loaded with ammunition in one direction and wounded and dead soldiers in the other.

Of course this frenzied activity didn't escape the Germans' notice. They sent scouts down into the corridors to map out the network of tunnels, but it wasn't an easy assignment. Even the few who managed to find their way out alive were unable to give an accurate description of the underground fortress.

The tunnels dead-ended just short of the German positions, so when the Allies launched their attack, they could blow open an exit and pop up right in the face of the surprised Germans.

The police officer's cousin, who didn't have too high an opinion of his native country and emigrated to America after the war, said the plan as General Allenby had devised it was ingenious, but the French ruined everything. First of all, they refused to fight on Easter Sunday, insisting that they had to celebrate the Resurrection. That meant the Allied attack, which was supposed to be coordinated with the offensive by General Nivelle along the river Aisne, had to be put off until Monday. Then, on Sunday night, it started to snow heavily. Vincent's supply unit should have been on their way inland by that point, but they had to wait until the storm let up.

The attack was planned for Monday morning at five-thirty.

A quiet set in after the evening bombing of the German trenches. The soldiers underground got a special dinner and the field chaplain celebrated Mass. Then they were ordered to go to bed so that they would be as well rested as possible for the next day. It wasn't hard to obey, given how tired they were. The boy in the bed next to Vincent's smiled blissfully and smacked his lips in his sleep.

But Vincent lay wide awake. He had never been so close to battle before. His perception of time was suddenly more acute, more intense, and the nearer it drew to morning, the more it slowed down, the minutes trickling by, draining away toward the beginning. Or was it the end? He savored the new sensation, every cell in his body up and on its feet as he eagerly lapped up the sounds around him: the tossing and turning, the scratching and moaning. A distant clapping, followed by a roar.

At first he thought the sound was coming from the kitchen, or from the generator that supplied power to the underground city. But then he realized what he was hearing were human voices. He got up, put on his glasses, grabbed his flashlight, and crept out to the corridor. He passed by the latrines on the right and came to the spot where the corridor widened into a tunnel. He continued a little farther toward the exit, then turned off into another corridor, where the noise and light were increasing in intensity.

He saw a group of about five men. Stomping heavily, they swayed from side to side, chanting in a barking voice, like a sudden exhalation of air. They moved in a circle around a lamp that served in place of a fire, their faces covered with Maori tattoos carved out of the darkness, the whites of their eyes bulging, tongues lolling from their mouths.

The soldiers rose at three-thirty in the morning. Everyone got a hot cup of coffee and a special ration of bread. Together, they prayed for victory and then, in full combat dress, arrayed for the assault. The snow was still falling outside, mixed with rain, and there was a strong wind blowing from the southwest—at the Allies' back and into the Germans' eyes.

Within a few minutes, they were already collecting the wounded in wheelbarrows. The first line of German trenches was captured almost without a hitch, having been reduced to a sea of craters in the Allied bombing the night before. Blinded by the sleet, the Germans failed to see the enemy approaching and weren't prepared to fight. Meanwhile the earth melted into a thick, sticky mud that sucked in their boots, so there was no way for them to flee. Some were taken hostage in their socks.

By evening time, the Allies had taken several strategic positions and the Germans were forced to retreat farther north. The Maori quickly laid down a makeshift road across the muddy battlefield to allow the ammunition and supplies to reach the front line.

The night before the battle and the whole following day, as he tugged the carts loaded with dead and wounded soldiers through the underground tunnels, were emblazoned in Vincent's memory as one of the most powerful experiences of the war.

He remembered the dying Englishman who had stopped in the midst of the attack to light his pipe when a grenade exploded in front of him. His head was unharmed, and he still had the pipe in his hand, but his chest was bleeding heavily. Vincent rushed the man to treatment as fast as he could, but he kept running into other carts carrying other wounded soldiers. The English soldier had a long, refined face with a high forehead and narrow nose, and a well-groomed mustache adorning his upper lip.

Seeing the Englishman moving his lips, Vincent leaned in close to listen.

"Helen . . ."

The policeman's cousin said it felt like the soldier was breathing his soul into his ear.

After the war he found out the Englishman's name, and looked up his wife in England. But that's another story.

"But what about the Red Baron?" asked Farouche. "Is that when he saw him?"

"Yes, that's right, his whole squadron. 'The Flying Circus,' they called them, because of their bright colors. They looked spectacular up in the sky. The British planes dropped over Arras like rotten plums."

The French policemen bid Andrei farewell on the Belgian border, explaining that they had to report back to Paris that evening or they would have escorted him all the way to Brussels.

Mssr. Després had arranged for Andrei to go to Brussels in order to salve his conscience. If he could make it to the capital and vanish amid the crowds, he had a chance of remaining at large. Even if personally Mssr. Després detested the idea of living in freedom illegally, he recognized that it was still preferable to languishing in a French prison.

5

HAVING THE OCEAN NEARBY makes everything softer. The late-afternoon light covers the flat landscape like a coating of honey.

By the time Andrei wakes up, it's dark. Squeezed into a corner of the compartment, he is nearly invisible. In his pocket he has his ticket to Brussels and the ten francs he had with him when he was arrested. The French policemen also left him the rest of a baguette, a hunk of cheese, and a half-empty bottle of wine.

He drifts off to sleep again. He is back home with his family in Vilnius, before they moved to Saint Petersburg. It is Yom Kippur and his father is taking him to temple. They lose each other in the crush outside the synagogue. He elbows his way through the crowd of men, all dressed in the same black outfits. Andrei wants to go home to his mother, but all of a sudden the streets look unfamiliar; he isn't in Vilnius anymore, but on the cramped, damp-smelling streets off the Bowery, in Manhattan. His ears buzz with the chatter of Jews on the sidewalk outside the synagogue.

He wakes up. Two men sit across from him, engaged in quiet conversation. Even in the darkness, he can make out their beards and black hats.

He closes his eyes and returns to the Bowery, no longer in

a dream, but in his memory. He climbs the stairs to the first apartment he rented in New York, with Louise and Sasha.

Sasha was his best friend. They found each other his first day in the city. Louise only joined them much later. She found her way to Manhattan by smell, with a single address in her pocket. She had run away from her husband and was just discovering anarchism. Although she was three years older than he was, in many respects he felt more mature.

Louise was his girl, but she sometimes also slept with Sasha. Andrei didn't mind too much; he took his principles seriously. He didn't own Louise. Besides which, he was genuinely fond of Sasha. While Andrei was out running around to meetings or editing at the offices of the German anarchist newspaper, Sasha, who was a painter, would sit around the kitchen at home, watching Louise cook and sew. They went through periods where all three of them lived off of the brassieres and corsets she made. The apartment was littered with padded inserts and pink ribbons. Sasha sat in the kitchen drawing or just stared dreamily at Louise with his bright blue eyes as he folded the satin cuttings into delicate roses.

The quiet conversation in Yiddish continues. The men, assuming Andrei to be asleep, are making fun of him.

"If he had a beard," says one, "he would look a lot like Grandpa Solomon. And Grandpa Solomon was born in Będzin."

"Look at his shoes," argues the other. "Can you imagine anyone from Będzin being caught dead in such shoes?"

"But he has the same nose as Grandpa Solomon. And the same ears, too."

"The world is full of such noses and ears."

Andrei suddenly shifts in his seat and the two men stop talking. But they keep their eyes glued to him. Their expression is not one of hostility, but curiosity.

"I was born in Vilnius and grew up in Saint Petersburg," Andrei says slowly. He remembers just enough Yiddish for a simple conversation. The men are overjoyed.

When did he leave Russia?

Is it true what they say, that the Bolsheviks are leaving the Jews alone?

Their mother's brother, Uncle Isaac, fled Ukraine with his family. The Bolsheviks there weren't murdering Jews, but they destroyed the synagogues and shut down the schools. They were teaching children to hate their fathers and not to believe in God.

"So what are you going to Antwerp for?" the two men ask.

"I'm not. I'm going to Brussels."

The men shake their heads with a smile. "You missed your stop. We got on in Brussels and this train is going to Antwerp."

So where was he coming from? And why?

Andrei gladly tells them everything. He always answers truthfully when people ask him questions. It's easier that way, he's found. Except for in jail. There he said nothing, no matter what they asked.

He shows them his ten francs.

"I don't know what I'll do," he says. "Maybe write a few letters and ask my friends to send me money. I need to get back to France."

"There is no legal way," says one of the men. "My guess is that they won't let you stay in Belgium, either."

"Where do you plan to sleep?" the other man asks.

"I have no idea." Andrei shrugs. "The train station?"

"They won't let you. You'll end up in jail, one two three."

"But you can come with us," the second man says, and the first one nods in agreement.

"Moishe," says the first man.

"Abel," the second man says, introducing himself.

"Moishe and Abel Kotler. Our shop is right across from the station. Maybe you know it."

ELEVEN YEARS LATER, Louise wrote this recollection of Andrei:

A grueling tug-of-war began with immigration officials after we left Russia. I resolved my status by entering into a pro forma marriage, but that was out of the question for Andrei. At one point, he was even expelled from France, and it was only through the intervention of influential friends that we succeeded in getting him back. The state apparatus knows how to get at its adversaries. Instead of Andrei writing or editing books and articles, he was filling out forms and exhausting himself standing in line at offices. I have no doubt that this humiliating struggle for a place on earth, which is the primary and inalienable right of every person, contributed to his decision to end his life prematurely.

In reality, Andrei's trail ended at the Antwerp train station, and none of the influential friends to whom Louise addressed her pleading letters offered any assistance. He was smuggled back into France by the diamond dealers Moishe and Abel Kotler.

6

OW EASY IT IS FOR THE STATE BUREAUCRACY to conspire against an individual who has become inconvenient. How easily one can dictate terms to a man who, even if he has given everything up, in the end still needs some space to live. "After my death," Andrei wrote in his will, "I wish to be cremated and have my ashes scattered. At least then I will no longer take up any space and I can escape from the cycle of applications, approvals, and rejections."

Bureaucracy had become such an integral part of their lives that Mimi, who had been too young to travel before the war, didn't even believe Andrei when he told her that in those days you didn't need any special permission to cross the border and settle down in another country. Mimi joined him in Paris once he returned from Belgium, and together they left for the south.

That was one of the conditions of his being allowed to reside in France: He had to move away from the capital and cease all political activity. He stopped work, at least openly, gave up his position as secretary of the fund for the relief of Russian political prisoners, and published his articles overseas, often under Louise's name. Louise had become a brand unto herself. Her name sold well. She had more requests to write than she could keep up with. Andrei also drew up the outlines for her lectures, and in return she sent him a percentage of the fees she received. He also promised to help her with her memoirs, and put off work on his own for the time being. His small household needed every franc it could get.

He and Mimi found a room with a kitchen on the ground floor of a house on rue de Gare, in Saint-Laurent-du-Var, a suburb of Nice.

Saint-Laurent was an independent commune with its own town hall and a downtown centered around the place Vieille, with streets so narrow that when you spread your arms you could easily touch the unplastered stone walls on either side. Rents were cheaper there than in the city. On Wednesday and Saturdays there was a market, and the beach was a short walk along the river Var. Not only that, but they had a yard of their own with a lemon tree and a miniature garden that Mimi was very proud of, where she grew parsley, basil, and thyme.

The only drawback compared to a larger city was that everyone in Saint-Laurent knew everyone else and they didn't like outsiders, even when they weren't nearly as suspicious as an elderly Jew with a limp, an accent, and a German mistress young enough to be his daughter.

MIMI HAD NEVER WANTED to get out of bed when they lived in Berlin, but here she rose at dawn, when the birds awakened her. She would creep into the kitchen and put water on for coffee. Then sweep the yard, water her herbs, and dash off to the baker's, all before Andrei opened his eyes. She loved the smell of Andrei's first cigarette, which he would smoke outdoors, with a mug of hot, sweet coffee in hand.

In summer they would walk to the beach early in the morning. Mimi would pack a basket with their breakfast, towels, a blanket, and pull on her swimsuit under her clothing. At around ten, when the sun began to get unpleasantly hot, they would go back home, close the shutters and open the windows to set up a breeze, and get down to work. Typically, Andrei would either write, edit, or translate, while Mimi looked up words in the dictionary, typed up his handwritten drafts, wrote letters, and, later, prepared lunch. After they ate, they would lie down for a bit before returning to work in the cool of the house and continuing through until the end of the afternoon. By that time there was shade in the yard and they could sit outside again. Just before sunset, they would make another trip to the sea. If they happened to be in the black, they would stop off at a bistro on their way back for a pastis, and if not, they would have some white wine at home. Their suppers were simple: bread, tomatoes, cheese, and fruit. At night they left the windows open, as well as the door that gave on to the yard. Mimi would listen to the buzzing of the cicadas and think about the stars. They seemed so incredibly close in the south, whereas in Berlin she had barely been able to see them. She bought herself a star map and learned the constellations. Everything about the seaside fascinated her: the plants, the fish, the recipes, the customs of the locals.

After the hustle and bustle of Berlin and their long separation, she finally had Andrei all to herself. They were already practically married. The only thing left was to go to town hall and make it official, but Andrei always had a reason to put it off. She had pressured him in Berlin, but now she didn't even mind so much that they weren't married, as long as he didn't leave her again. Taking care of him, she was peaceful and happy. Here the ghosts of Berlin—friends and especially former lovers—were safely far away. All Andrei could do was write to them.

7

ANDREI HAD BEEN CONSTANTLY IN DEMAND in Berlin. Guests had come calling at all hours, even after midnight. He would brew tea, pour wine, and argue politics, all still in his pajamas. Mimi couldn't stand when people "interfered with Andrei's rest," but there was no escaping it. In Saint-Laurent, on the other hand, they made it through almost the whole first summer without a single visitor.

Then, as a harbinger of change to come, Nancy Harwood literally appeared on the horizon. An American oil heiress married to drinker and gambler Jack Harwood. A millionairess who divided her time between Paris and the Côte d'Azur and whose scandals filled the gossip columns on a regular basis.

It was eight in the morning. Mimi had just gone for a swim and was stretched out in the sun. Andrei lay on his side, head propped in his hand, smoking a cigarette as he gazed out at the sea. They could track the passing of time by the shadow of Andrei's cane, plunged upright in the sand. The beach and promenade were almost empty. Guests were just waking up in the hotels along the coast. Nothing but open space in every direction. Sailboats were setting out from the port of Saint-Laurent, white birds drowned in a sea of blue, vanishing over the horizon, slowly or quickly, depending on how strong the wind was blowing.

Andrei was speaking, half to Mimi, half to himself. "Rosa

Luxemburg was wrong. I was wrong. Man can't be reduced to his role in the hierarchy of economic relations. The problem lies elsewhere. Money is just a derivative evil. It isn't enough to change the economic order! Whether it's God or the state, we have to abolish the patriarchal apparatus. As we found out in Russia, it can't be destroyed by violence. One power system just replaces the other. We have to declare disobedience to it, ignore it, mentally dissolve it. Stop playing the game!"

Andrei sat up in excitement. "Mimi, I figured it out!"

One of the sailboats was coming toward them. Already it was close enough for them to decipher the name of the boat, spelled out in white against the red hull: FIREFLY.

"Any farther," said Andrei, "and it's going to run aground."

The captain must have realized the same thing, because he dropped anchor and the crew began taking in the sails. Mimi watched the sailors at work, counting three of them on board; then she noticed a female figure dressed in white who had climbed onto the railing and was waving both hands and shouting something.

The idyll was over. Mimi could feel it in her gut. She was ready to pack her things and run away, but Andrei had other plans. She looked at him: shading his eyes with his hand, watching the woman on the railing with curiosity. He was smiling.

"Who could that be?" Mimi asked.

With one swift movement, the woman pulled her dress over her head, tossed it onto the deck, executed a graceful swan dive into the water, and began swimming to shore.

Andrei sat up in anticipation, then propped himself up to a standing position with the help of his cane and walked toward the water's edge. Mimi wondered whether he had known the

Firefly was coming. It seemed like he and the woman had some kind of arrangement.

"Who is that?" Mimi asked again.

Andrei shrugged and stepped into the water.

The woman was a good swimmer. Within a few minutes, she was wading through the shallows toward Andrei, breathing heavily, but with a smile on her face. She was young, tall, and thin, with a tanned, athletically toned body. Her short brown hair was plastered to her skull. She held out her hand to Andrei. "Nancy. Nancy Harwood. We knew you would be here. You must be Andrei. I read your *Notes from Prison*. Quite remarkable, if I may say so."

Andrei took her hand and squeezed it affectionately.

From where she sat, Mimi could hear every word. Like every American she had met, this one was very loud.

"We set sail from Saint-Tropez last night," Nancy said. "And we have a pleasant surprise for you. At least I hope it will be pleasant. Besides that, we have plenty of champagne on board. Will you join us for a glass? Or have you already had breakfast?"

She laughed at her own joke, and just kept laughing and laughing.

Andrei waved to Mimi. "Come here."

Mimi didn't move. She didn't want to drink champagne with strangers. She wasn't curious about their surprise. She didn't like the woman. There was something dangerous about her. The way she flattered Andrei. And Andrei, who normally couldn't stand flattery, didn't raise a word of objection. From the looks of it, he enjoyed it. Him and his women, Mimi thought angrily to herself.

Andrei waved to her again. She would have to go meet this vulgar American woman.

A small dinghy detached itself from the side of the sailboat. There were two people sitting in it: a man, and a woman in a straw hat with a red ribbon. The woman was waving.

"That's the surprise." Nancy theatrically unfurled a long, tanned arm. "We've brought you your girlfriend."

"I thought she was still in Canada," said Andrei, shaking his head in delight. "Why didn't she write?"

"It wouldn't have been a surprise then," said Nancy.

THE MAN AT THE OARS is Nancy's husband, Jack. He anchors the boat in the sandy shallows, rolls up the legs of his linen summer trousers, and makes his way to shore, in one hand a basket of food, in the other a bucket of ice with three bottles of champagne sticking out of it. As Andrei helps Louise from the boat, she plunks into the water, soaking her skirt up to the waist. She has aged even more in the two years since he last saw her. Her hair now is totally gray, and she has also put on weight. But she laughs, giving Andrei a hug like in the old days, and addresses him as "boy."

"So, my boy, how are you doing here?"

Once on shore, she greets Mimi, spreads out her skirt on the sand to dry, and delivers the news that Nancy has bought her a house in Saint-Tropez, a beautiful little villa on a hill overlooking the sea, with a garden and a small patch of vineyard. That means there are no more obstacles to keep her from starting work on her memoirs. She has a place to write now, and finally, too, she'll have her own home. She also has the resources, since her friends took up a collection, so she can pay Andrei, too. She's counting on him to help with the writing. She's already started sending out letters. There are so many facts to verify, old documents to request.

Nancy and Jack leave them alone to talk in peace. They can entertain themselves just fine. Nancy lies on her stomach, playing with a glass of wine. She has buried it in the sand and circled it with a ring of shells. Jack reads the newspaper, smoking.

Nobody paid any attention to Mimi. Louise had always looked right through her. In Berlin, she had treated her as nothing but an appendage of Andrei, someone who had to be counted only when setting the table. Louise didn't take any of Andrei's lovers seriously. She classified them all either as pampered princesses or secretaries, which in her experience were even worse. But she couldn't be jealous of them. She had known Andrei too long for that. His lovers were interchangeable.

Mimi could sense all of this, which was why she didn't like Louise. She wasn't Andrei's lover, she was his wife, whether or not they had a paper saying so. Andrei belonged to her, and even Louise had to accept that.

Nancy finishes her drink and sits up. She crawls over to Jack on her knees, wraps her long arms around his neck, and gives him a kiss on the ear.

Jack bristles. "You're covered in sand."

She sticks out her chest. "Then clean me."

"Oh, stop it. Why don't you put some clothes on."

Nancy turns away, dejected.

"So where are we going for lunch?" Jack yawns.

8

IT WAS A LONG DAY. By the time they finally got home, around sunup, Mimi felt several years older. She was tired, dirty, and filled with tears she had been holding in.

It started with lunch on the terrace at the Hotel Imperial (the white-coated waiters pretended not to notice Mimi's old summer dress, in which she had run to the beach that morning) and ended with an exhausting trek from bar to bar.

The more they drank, the darker Jack turned, and at three o'clock in the morning, at the Blind Dog bistro, with the electric fans spinning lazily on the ceiling, he flung himself on Nancy. He would have beaten her to a pulp if Andrei hadn't stepped in. The only other people there besides them were a couple of prostitutes with their pimps, and they weren't about to get involved. They were used to scenes like that.

"She's a whore," Jack told Andrei as Louise rocked the sobbing Nancy in her massive arms. "And ugly besides. And whose fault is that? Dr. Schrer from Minnesota. Go ahead, ask her, she'll tell you. Stupid bitch! Dumbest millionaire I know. You know what that doctor did to her? He promised to cut off a piece of her nose, then didn't do it. He just left it the way it was. Didn't want to lay a hand on little Nini's schnoz. Little Nini, you know that's what they used to call her at home? Now she's got to live with a nose like a cucumber for the rest of her life, poor girl. Can you imagine? People are dying of hunger and little Nini's all upset about her nose. What can comfort her now, except champagne and cocaine? Just ask, she'll tell you herself. Little Nini wants to be loved. Admired. But not for her money." Jack laughed. "As long as you're making eyes at everyone, why don't you just go right ahead and strip?" He reached across the table, grabbed a handful of Nancy's silk dress, and ripped it in half down to her waist. Nancy was too stunned to try to hide her tiny white breasts. She just went on crying while Louise took off her summer scarf and wrapped her up in it.

Andrei ran outside to find a taxi. The *Firefly* was anchored in the harbor. Louise said she could sleep on the boat with Nancy and Jack and sail back to Saint-Tropez with them the next day.

Having reduced Nancy to tears, Jack finally calmed down. He was in a good mood again for the first time since morning. He moved over next to Mimi and pressed up against her, wrapping one hand around her shoulders and resting the other on her thigh.

"Come back to the boat with me," he whispered. "I'll show you my cabin. Nancy'll sleep like a log. I know her. Your eyes are so . . . blue."

Andrei came back with a taxi and they all walked out together. Jack kept a tight grip on Mimi's hand; she couldn't get away. He pulled her into the open car, but Andrei didn't notice. He was too busy talking to Louise, who was propping up Nancy.

"Will you stay the night with me and Mimi?" he asked.

"I need to get home," said Louise.

"That's no problem. You can go back tomorrow by train or boat."

Nancy shook her head. "Louise is coming with us. Aren't you, Louise darling?"

"I can't leave her alone with him," said Louise.

"Oh, thank you." Nancy gave her a hug.

"Nancy, dear, how long do you plan to put up with this? Don't you see how he's humiliating you?"

"He just has these fits."

"But they're practically every day."

"Then tell me," said Nancy. "Tell me what to do. I love Jack. You too, darling Louise. You're my . . . pillar. Pleasure to meet you," Nancy said, letting go of Louise to give Andrei a hug. "We'll see each other soon. We'll bring Louise for you again, won't we, Louise? But for now, we have to take her with us. Good-bye." She turned to Mimi. "What was your name again?"

"Emma Stein," said Mimi, who had finally managed to wrench herself free from Jack. "My name is Emma Stein." Then, at last, they were gone.

ANDREI AND MIMI WALK HOME the rest of the way. Andrei doesn't want to go to bed yet, so he sits in the yard and smokes, watching the brightening sky.

"She bought Louise a house," he says, thinking out loud. "She must be extremely grateful to her. He's a real monster, though. As for her, she's got too much money. Other than that, she's quite nice, don't you think?"

No answer.

"Mimi?"

He hears a sob from the bedroom.

Sighing, Andrei extinguishes his cigarette, gets up, and walks into the dark bedroom. He sits down on the edge of the bed and finds Mimi's smooth, round face with his hand. She jerks away from him.

"What is wrong with you, Mimi? I thought you got over your jealousy and left the green-eyed monster behind in Berlin. Now it lives comfortably on its pension, visiting the zoo with its grandchildren, and has no reason to bother Mimi anymore, does it?"

"Stop," Mimi blurts. "Everything's ruined."

"No, it's not."

"Yes, it is. Now *she's* here and she's going to want you back for herself, you'll see. I don't think I can take it."

"Of course you can."

"You don't love me."

"I do."

"Then marry me."

"Mimi, come on. We've been through this before. I thought you understood why I don't believe in marriage."

"You and your principles!"

"I don't have any principles. I just don't want anyone interfering in our private matters. At least when it comes to this. Mimi, let's keep it just between us, all right?"

"But I want to be your wife. I want Louise to have to accept it. And my family, too."

"That's all that matters to you."

"I love you," says Mimi. "You're my first and only love."

He strokes her hair, wet with sweat and tears. "Poor Mimi."

9

I T TOOK LOUISE TWO YEARS TO WRITE her memoirs. Two stormy years, in the course of which Mimi began to have stomach problems and Andrei developed a painful boil on his chest that refused to heal.

As Louise finished each chapter, she would send it through the mail to Andrei, who would revise and rewrite, and once he had accumulated a large enough number of them, he would personally deliver them to Louise. He would always end up spending a few days in Saint-Tropez, during which he had to leave Mimi on her own. It made no sense to take her with him, not to mention that Louise was paying for the ticket. It was purely a business trip, and most of the time it wasn't even that nice, with Louise fighting him over each and every word. His insistence on accuracy irritated her no end.

"These are my personal memoirs," she yelled at him, "not the annals of anarchism!"

Andrei disagreed. "They're both. That's why the book is so important. Write whatever you want about your lovers, but the facts have to be correct. Otherwise they'll tear you apart. And as far as style goes, try to describe things a little bit more from the outside, instead of just as you see them."

"Are you saying I'm egocentric?"

"Don't take everything so personally, Louise."

She did take it personally, and even though in the end they

always parted as friends, she couldn't forgive him. Andrei would leave her home completely drained. Not only that, but he did the last revisions for next to nothing, since the money Louise had rounded up to support herself while she was writing was running out. That meant he, in turn, had to scrape together even more translation and editing work, but he felt responsible for Louise's memoirs.

There was a constant stream of guests through the house in Saint-Tropez, mostly old friends from America, who for one reason or another were now living in France, and of course they wanted to get together with both Louise and Andrei. Gone was the peace and quiet of their first summer, and the little household in Saint-Laurent grew gloomier by the day.

"Why don't you come with me?" Andrei said when Mimi reproached him for leaving her alone again.

"None of your friends like me."

"That's because you mope around like a sourpuss all the time. And besides, that's not true."

"Yes, it is. I can tell. Louise thinks I'm stupid."

"Certainly not. She just thinks you shouldn't be so jealous. Especially when it comes to her."

"Do the two of you talk about me?"

"Not particularly."

"I can't stand the way you talk to Nancy and all those other women. The way your friends look right through me." Mimi was crying. "Would you rather be with someone else?"

"No."

"Then why do you leave me alone all the time?"

"Because you don't want to go anywhere."

Their landlady lived upstairs with her husband. She couldn't understand their arguments, so she could only guess at why she heard crying and screaming from downstairs so often. She assumed it was jealousy. Probably the old Jew jealous of his young girlfriend.

Andrei and Mimi would argue late into the night, and when Mimi's screaming got too loud, the landlady would call the police. Not that she needed to, but it gave her the chance to get a peek inside the anarchist household.

LOUISE'S MEMOIRS WERE PUBLISHED as a two-volume work, and the reviews were surprisingly positive, even from outlets that were traditionally hostile. The only ones who tore her apart were the Communists. Andrei said that could mean only one thing: Louise was no longer dangerous to America. The country's war on anarchists had ended with their deportation. Not that they would take her back, but like every high-profile enemy whose day had passed, Louise became a national mascot nearly overnight. Her publisher secured a visa for her so she could go on a book tour, and it was a major success. Louise ignited the same spark in her listeners as she had in her youth, and even though she was officially prohibited from speaking about anything not directly connected to her memoirs, wherever she appeared, it turned into a spontaneous demonstration of anarchism. After a long period of doubt, she once again felt she had made the right choice in her life and that her ideals had meaning not only for her.

She wrote about it to Andrei, who replied:

Yes, it is precisely that need to have an ideal to fight for, which every member of the human species shares in common, that I see as our only hope. The fact that it has usually been a bad ideal of no benefit to anyone—be it religion, nation, or personal honor—is another matter. But if humanity could get behind an ideal that was good, we could enjoy the greatest prosperity in our history. I have lost hope in the ability of enlightened individuals to bring about change directly. Enlightened individuals are always in the minority and can't achieve anything except through the intermediary of a state apparatus. We saw how that turned out in Russia.

As to your question of whether or not I would like to try to get a visa to America, the answer is no. Thank you for the offer of help, but believe me, I'm being honest when I say I have lost interest. Or, to be more accurate, my interest in America is spent.

The next letter from Louise brought more news: She was in Chicago. And she was in love.

10

MARTIN BRUNSCHWIG HAD BEEN BLIND since childhood. With his right eye, he could make out light, dark, and shapes; with his left, he saw nothing at all. With his mother reading to him, he was able to study law and become a lawyer, a profession in which blindness was no obstacle. Whereas before, his mother had accompanied him everywhere, now he looked out at the world through the eyes of his young wife, who viewed her service to him as her mission in life. Together, they helped people who couldn't afford other lawyers, going to court on behalf of abandoned mothers, widows, war veterans, immigrants, and the unemployed.

Martin was intrigued by anarchism—in his opinion, the only social theory based on human goodness. Having read Kropotkin and loved Tolstoy, he was thrilled when he heard that Louise would be giving a public presentation on her book. His wife had read long passages of it to him, and he had been taken by the strange flickering between the lines.

Louise was the embodiment of his ideal, he told his wife: passionate, wise, unfettered by convention, a woman who could uplift a man and liberate him from the banality of the everyday.

They sat down in the front row, so his wife could describe Louise to him.

"Shorter than me, full-figured, with gray hair pulled up in

a bun. She's wearing round wire-rimmed glasses, and a light blouse with a round collar and a beige skirt."

When it came time for questions, Martin raised his hand. "You have such a rich, interesting life." (He said *have*, not *had*, Louise noticed.) "Are you happy?"

There was a long silence before she spoke. "I'm happy that I'm here. When I see and hear your support, the enthusiasm young people have for an ideal for which I sacrificed my life. But when this meeting is over and I go back to my hotel room, alone again, with nobody waiting for me, it isn't exactly . . ." Her voice trailed off into silence.

When the talk was over, Martin asked his wife to take him up to see Louise.

"I shouldn't have asked you such a personal question," he said. "I apologize for embarrassing you. The truth is, I'm blind, so I forgot it wasn't just the two of us and there were hundreds of other people in the room, listening as closely as I was. I hope you understand." He quickly added, "I would gladly wait for you in that room, if you would let me."

Louise remained silent.

"Do you think I'm ridiculous?" Martin asked.

"No."

"Then would you be willing to make some time for me? May I speak with you in private?"

She glanced at Martin's wife, who looked like a child still. A slim, pretty blonde with a friendly face, she nodded and gave Louise a pleading look, as if she were the one asking for an audience, not her husband.

"I'm busy today, but why don't you come by for tea

tomorrow afternoon? With your wife, of course." She smiled at the girl.

"No," Martin said. "I'll come alone. Could you write down the address, please?"

She dictated the address of her hotel to Martin's wife, shook hands with both of them, and moved on to the next in the long line of readers waiting for her.

LOUISE WAS IN HER SIXTIES. Martin was half her age. After what she had been through with Lars, she stayed away from younger men. She didn't have the strength to go through all that again. Letting herself be talked into the impossible, only to watch the look in his eyes change as the romantic fantasy inevitably faded away into everyday life. No longer did he see before him the legendary Louise G., but an aging woman, entertaining for a night on the town perhaps, debating politics over a glass of whiskey and cigarettes, but best left to her own bed.

The worst part was, on the inside, Louise didn't feel any different. Andrei had confided in her that his sexual needs had diminished with age. "It must be disappointing for a young woman like Mimi," he said. "It's true she didn't have any experience before me, so she has nothing to compare to. Not like those women who insist on giving a man a test run first. Still, her patience, and the fact that she doesn't complain, are further evidence of a selflessness I find moving."

Instead of relief, aging brought Louise only fewer opportunities. In the summer she suffered the most. Rolling around on her bed in heat, cursing nature for punishing women. No wonder the Jews had invented Eve and her sin, she thought. How else to explain the injustice!

After two meetings (one drinking tea together, the next strolling in the park), it was obvious that Martin expected something from her. After Boston she was headed to Chicago, where her plan was to relax in a house borrowed from friends and work on a long article a newspaper in New York had commissioned from her. Before they said their good-byes, he asked whether he might come to Chicago to see her. He had never traveled alone by train, but he was sure he could manage if she met him at the station.

She refused; he insisted. He had to meet her again.

She said she would think about it.

Happily, Martin gave her a hug and kissed her on the lips. She held his blond-haired head in her hands, thinking about the fact that he couldn't see her.

When Lars left her, she had vowed to herself never again to love a younger man. Even if a thousand serpents of Paradise seduced her, she never wanted to experience that feeling of despair and ingratitude again. That unsparing look directed at her by all her young lovers, sooner or later. No night was dark enough to disguise it.

At least there's no risk of that with him, Louise thought, stroking Martin's hair. She was hungry for love, for the intimate words and caresses.

AFTER THREE DAYS IN CHICAGO, Louise still couldn't make up her mind whether or not to invite Martin. In two weeks her visa would expire, and she would have to return to Canada and apply for a new one. On the morning of the fourth day, a letter arrived in the mail. Written to her in tiny, neat lettering by Martin's wife.

"Dear Madam," it said, "you may not realize what a deep impression you have made on my husband. He needs you, to be near you and your influence. You cannot imagine how he suffers. Please let him come see you. I have no feeling of ownership toward Martin the way other wives do toward their husbands. He is an extraordinary person, with both extraordinary abilities and extraordinary needs. If he feels that he can learn something important from you, I have no right to stand in his way. Whatever he experiences, I experience, too. We have no secrets between us, no boundaries it is forbidden to cross. Perhaps you, of all people, may understand that our trust in each other is founded on absolute freedom. Martin asked me to write you, as it occurred to him that even such an enlightened being as yourself may hesitate out of considerations which in our case are truly secondary. Please, Madam Louise, assuming you don't find my husband disagreeable, let him come. You will be enriching not only his life, but mine."

Martin added just four words: "May I come now?"

She waited for him at the station and took him home.

Martin wanted to wash up and change clothes after the long journey, and being in a strange environment, he needed help. This offered a natural route to physical intimacy. As Louise tended to him, he reciprocated her caresses. He knew what she looked like, but that wasn't important to him; he had never cared for surfaces. There was so much joy in Louise's love! Over and over he told her how he felt no difference in age between them.

Louise had to hold herself back to keep from going out of her mind. The more she stuck to her daily routine, the easier it would be to cope with the inevitable loss. Every afternoon she set aside at least a few hours for writing; the rest of the day they spent together. It was so good, there was no need to think about it. She accepted the ten days as a reward for her long years of solitude, recognizing their exceptional beauty more acutely than she would have in her youth.

Before she left, they vowed to each other to meet again soon. As soon as she renewed her visa, she would return to America and they would go on a trip together. Louise would take Martin with her on a lecture tour. Show him California, where he had never been. Introduce him to the southern sun and the Pacific Ocean. He didn't have to see it, she said. It was enough just to hear the roar and pound of the waves, to feel the freezing spray on your face and breathe in the fresh salty smell.

But the U.S. Immigration Service had other plans for Louise, and this time even a guarantee from the publisher didn't help. The reports from the police who had monitored her lectures were unequivocal: Louise G. had failed to comply with the conditions stated in her visa and had used her appearances as a pretext for political agitation. Her continued presence in the United States was undesirable.

"The dream is over," Louise wrote to Andrei. "Martin is asking if he can come see me in Canada or Saint-Tropez, but for obvious reasons, I can't allow it."

11

VISITORS FROM AMERICA CAME AND WENT, pledging to help, but Louise's visa applications were repeatedly rejected. She refused to accept that she would never see home again. Home for her was New York. First the apartment on the Bowery, then the small house in Harlem with the magazine offices on the ground floor, where Andrei had lived when he got out of prison.

Andrei didn't share her feelings. Postwar America no longer held any interest for him and he didn't feel at home anywhere. He had never owned anything, never settled in anywhere. He answered to a higher calling and lived where necessary.

Despite the official harassment, in France at least he was still connected to Russia. He could collect aid for political prisoners and their families from a distance and edit the newsletter, which reported on the ideas and fates of imprisoned anarchists. That was the best he could do at the moment, he felt. He wouldn't allow the imprisoned and executed anarchists to be forgotten; he wouldn't allow their sacrifice to be in vain. It was up to him to preserve the evidence of how the Bolsheviks had stolen the revolution, leaving Russia under the control of a band of opportunists, who not only didn't care about ideals but quietly sought to get rid of the true idealists as quickly as possible.

Andrei hadn't lapsed into despair like Louise. He didn't think the rise of fascism and Nazism in Europe proved the futility of their lifelong efforts. He believed that the evolution of humanity needed to be viewed in a broader context, rather than on the scale of a single human life. They were working for the benefit of the future, and none of it was in vain. Each and every human being mattered. Any person who consciously refused to rule and be ruled represented a distinct change for the better.

It was true that at a certain point in history—just before the outbreak of war—it had looked like anarchism might become a mass movement. But it didn't happen. There was no choice but to accept it, to withdraw modestly to the sidelines and continue the work, without letting up, maintaining a clear vision. After the night that had now fallen over Europe, daylight would come again. Humanity would survive, as it had survived all the horrors up to now, and once again people would search for an ideal.

AFTER SHE CAME BACK FROM CANADA, Louise's brain was like a broken record, repeating over and over: Why bother? Whom and what was it for?

Maybe having children would have helped. Nature had made the choice easy for her. She would have had to undergo an operation to get pregnant when she was younger. Faced with the same situation today, she still would have made the same decision, but knowing that didn't take away the bitter taste of growing old and being on her own. She felt cheated. She had expected a reward for her sacrifice, but none was forthcoming. The world had suddenly changed course, leaving her by the wayside. Or had she already received her reward, and was now paying it back?

Andrei accused her of vanity. The vanity of old age, no less! He argued that she was wasting her time trying to reach a wider audience, and succumbing to the influence of flatterers. They hadn't spoken to each other for several weeks in Berlin because Andrei had wanted her to publish her account of Russia with an anarchist press instead of a commercial house that would sell it at an unaffordable price to make a profit. His fears, unfortunately, were confirmed when the publisher removed the whole last part of the book and changed the title without Louise's knowledge.

She wanted Andrei to come see her more often, and tried to lure him to Saint-Tropez by setting up a room just for him, with a beautifully colored bedspread and a desk with a view of the vineyard. She could cook for him, and he would have peace and quiet.

He did come, occasionally, but he would just sleep over and then rush right home. Mimi threw tantrums over the phone. Where does Andrei get the patience to deal with her jealous outbursts? wondered Louise. How could he love a woman who is so openly hostile to me?

Louise tried to make friends with Mimi, but it always turned out the same. After a few polite letters, something would go awry and Mimi would find an excuse to be jealous. Also, her stomach problems were getting worse. She would have seizures, rolling around on the ground, moaning in pain. The doctors weren't sure what it was. Louise thought she was just doing it to blackmail Andrei. Even worse, Andrei himself wasn't healthy. It hurt when he urinated, and he was probably going to need an operation.

12

L ATE JUNE. A LIGHT WEST WIND RIPPLES the water's surface in the morning, but by afternoon not a leaf stirs, and the sea, green at the edges, turning a dark blue toward the horizon, lies still as a heat-stricken beast.

Saturday morning, Saint-Tropez

Dear boy,
On this day I am doubly sorry that you aren't here.

I sit in your room, writing at your desk, looking out at the vineyard in the morning sun, and I want to tell you: However hard my life has been, whatever disappointment it has brought me, especially in recent years, one thing is certain. The friendship I feel for you is the only thing I have left. Men have come and gone. Some I loved; you know that. But none of them has been so completely intertwined with every fiber of my being as you.

I have become accustomed to the losses. I am slowly coming to terms with the fact that my life, like everyone else's, has turned out to be nothing like what I had imagined. The only loss with which I cannot come to terms, the only true disaster that could befall me, would be to lose you. Or your friendship.

I am sad and my head feels swept clean of thoughts. There is nothing there except this: Andrei, my dear boy, is feeling better, the pain has subsided, the operation was a success, and even though he

*cannot be with me on the day of my birth, he is getting better and
we will see each other soon.*

*Greetings to Mimi. I changed my opinion of her somewhat
when I saw how brave and selfless she was in taking care of you.
Seeing as I cannot. Seeing as you, my boy, will not allow me to.*

*I hope we shall soon see each other. That would be the best
belated birthday present I could have.*

Yours, L.

Saturday morning, Saint-Laurent

Dear girl,
*Pardon my chicken scratch, but I am writing lying down, with
Mimi helping me. I am unable to come and celebrate your birthday with you this year, but I think of you constantly and send
you my warmest greetings. Although I am doing noticeably better,
travel is, unfortunately, still out of the question. Have a good celebration without us, say hello to all our friends, and don't be sad.
Surely better times will come again, perhaps not in our lifetime,
but what difference does it make?*

*Mimi and I are with you in spirit. I will call you later this
evening to offer more personal greetings.*

Yours, A.

The letters, which crossed paths somewhere near Antibes,
failed to reach their addressees in time. Louise didn't receive
Andrei's belated message until Wednesday evening, after her
return home. She found it tucked under the door, and when
she saw Andrei's writing on the envelope, she forgot for a
moment where she was coming from and why.

13

ANDREI KEPT HIS PROMISE and on Saturday evening called Louise. She told him that if Muhammad couldn't come to the mountain, the mountain would come to Muhammad. In other words, she would travel to Saint-Laurent the next morning.

Andrei tried to talk her out of it. He still wasn't feeling that well; it would be better for them to wait until he was back in shape a little. Mimi was taking exemplary care of him, not to worry.

"Do you need any money?" Louise asked bluntly. They were both hardened warriors. There was no need for them to pretend in front of each other.

It wasn't urgent at the moment, said Andrei. He had recently received some funds from England. Though it was true, after paying the hospital bills, they wouldn't have too much left.

She promised to send some money on Monday.

Andrei had undergone a second operation on his prostate. The first one had only made it worse, but the doctors promised relief this time, just as soon as the scar tissue and bruises had healed.

Getting him home was the worst. He was in too much pain to move. He felt utterly miserable. Mimi saw him at his moment of greatest weakness. She cleaned up his feces, urine, and blood. She held his head in the ambulance as he bit his hand in pain, calling on all the saints for help in his native Russian.

They gave him a bottle of laudanum to take home with him, which dampened the pain a little, but how long would it last him for? Where would they get the money for medicine? Why should Mimi have to beg from her family and friends and sacrifice herself for an invalid who wouldn't produce anything of any worth again and probably couldn't even make love to her anymore?

He took the last dose of laudanum on Saturday afternoon. That evening, shortly after his phone call with Louise, the effect wore off and the pain set in with redoubled strength. He was too tired. It didn't make any sense.

"Go fetch the doctor," he told Mimi. "Run."

"I can't leave you here," she said.

"You have to. I need . . . something. This is unbearable."

"I can't," she said.

"Go, by all the saints, run! Go and find him."

She ran sobbing from the room.

Doubled over in pain, he shuffled over to his desk and slid open the middle drawer.

He had carried a pistol with him ever since he got out of prison in Pittsburgh. In his view, the option to end one's own life was a fundamental freedom, the only one he had left. What with all the financial hardship, being pushed around from place to place, and now his sickness on top of it, the loaded gun was his one assurance. Mimi and Louise both knew; he didn't keep it a secret. The moment his suffering became too much to bear and the difficulties of surviving came to outweigh the positives of life, he wouldn't hesitate. In Russia, the Bolsheviks had accused him of sentimentality, but that was only when it came to others. He felt no special attachment toward himself. He had already given up everything once before in his youth. In that respect, he had been free ever since.

He wrote down a few words of explanation on a sheet of paper and went back to bed with the gun. He didn't want Mimi to see right away what had happened.

He pressed the mouth of the gun to the soft spot under his breastbone to avoid hitting his rib cage. He aimed upward and a little to the left. Only a few inches of soft tissue separated his heart from the bullet. There was no way he could miss. He gasped for breath as blood rushed into his throat. The pistol fell from his hand. He couldn't reach down to pick it up and fire another shot. He lay curled in a ball on his left side, still alive.

Back then, too, he had aimed at the heart and missed. Kolman, who was smaller than he had imagined, had fallen under the desk and started crawling toward the window, where particles of dust swirled in a splotch of sunlight. Someone had come running in and pounced on Andrei's back. As he tumbled to the floor, he had pulled a knife from his pocket and stabbed Kolman in the leg. Killing is terrible business.

Mimi didn't notice anything when she got back. Andrei had stopped moaning. Maybe the pain had let up.

The doctor, who walked in the door right behind her, noticed the discarded revolver under the bed and sent Mimi into the kitchen. He pulled away the blanket, put it back again, and walked into the kitchen. "Do you have a phone?" he asked Mimi.

"We go to the neighbors' to call," she said.

"Don't bother him for now. I gave him a shot so he could

sleep. Why don't you lie down for a while, too," the doctor said, and walked out the door.

First he called the ambulance, then the police.

Mimi was shaken awake from her short, exhausted sleep to see Andrei being loaded into the ambulance.

"You're coming with us," said the younger of the two local gendarmes, clicking the handcuffs around her wrists.

"You're under arrest," the other declared. "Anything you say can be used against you."

"I don't understand," Mimi said, shaking her head. "Who called the ambulance? Where are they taking him?"

"You have some explaining to do."

"But what is this about?"

"Murder," said the younger gendarme.

They took her to the police station.

The only thing Mimi could recall amid the shock was Louise's telephone number. Andrei had drummed it into her head for so long, she couldn't forget.

"If anything should happen to me," he had told her, "call Louise immediately. Do you hear?"

"But why Louise?"

"Believe it or not, Louise is our most loyal friend, both of us, you and me. She's capable, and we can rely on her. If anything happens to me, she'll help you out."

"May I make a phone call?" Mimi asked the older gendarme.

"Be my guest." He unlocked the handcuffs and pushed the telephone across the desk to her. He studied her closely as she dialed the number with a trembling finger and stammered into the ear of a still-sleepy Louise that she needed to come immediately.

LOUISE ARRIVED LATE SUNDAY MORNING. She began the journey at 3:00 A.M., after Mimi called, but she had to wait for the first bus and change twice along the way. She ran straight to the hospital. Andrei recognized her, but he was in too much pain to speak. The bullet had passed through his stomach and left lung and lodged itself in his spine. The damage was too extensive for them to operate. There was nothing to do but wait for the end and pray that it would come soon.

Mimi sat on the opposite side of the bed from Louise, gripping Andrei's cool, sweaty hands in hers. The police had kept her at the station as long as they could, but in the morning they'd had to let her go. Two independent doctors, including a police expert, had declared Andrei's wounds to be a clear case of attempted suicide, and a search of the room had produced Andrei's farewell letter: "Mimi, honey, forgive me. You too, Louise. I don't want to live dependent on others. Louise, help Mimi. Love, A."

14

"LOUISE'S BRAIN IS A CONSTANT SOURCE of amazement to me." Louise clapped shut Andrei's diary. No, she didn't want to read it right now.

She and Mimi had spent the night with friends. The doctors gave Mimi a shot of sedatives, so she slept peacefully, face turned to the wall. Louise sat for a long time out on the balcony, smoking, but then she too took a pill. She had a busy day ahead of her. She and Mimi had to clean up the house and arrange the funeral. And after the funeral she would have to take Mimi to Saint-Tropez. She couldn't be left alone right now.

She blamed herself for not coming sooner. She shouldn't have listened to Andrei. It might not have happened if Mimi hadn't been alone with him.

How could he do that to her? What could he have been thinking?

The next morning she went into the house first, leaving Mimi to sit in the yard. The kitchen looked like it always did, nothing out of the ordinary. At first glance nothing was out of place in the bedroom either, just a rumpled bed covered with a blanket. She decided to leave the blanket on and pack up the mattress, together with the sheet and covers, tie the whole thing up, and carry it outside.

Mimi sat quietly beneath the lemon tree. When Louise

called out to ask if she could find or borrow a ball of twine, she got up and went to the landlords'.

Mimi came back with the twine and the landlady, who insisted on helping them. She said she had wanted to clean the apartment herself, before they came back, but she hadn't been sure if Mimi would mind. Also, the police had been there. When they left, she had wiped up the blood on the floor and covered the bed with a blanket.

"Oh, my dear sweet girl," the landlady cried, giving Mimi a hug. The same Mimi she had gossiped about all over town, asking why on earth a girl would want to live with a man old enough to be her father.

"What are you going to do, now that you're on your own?"

Mimi broke free of her arms with a look of alarm on her face. She sensed she was in danger but didn't quite understand how.

The landlady helped Louise tie up the mattress and covers and then called her husband, who dragged in a cart and, with a lot of grunting and panting, loaded up the package and hauled it uphill to the village dump.

Before she left, the landlady asked Louise for the last two months' rent and reimbursement for the ruined mattress and bedding. She said she realized it wasn't the right time, but she hoped Louise would understand. Mimi might disappear, leaving her debts unpaid.

Once the owner had left, Mimi stretched out on the sofa in the kitchen and closed her eyes. Louise, with her permission, opened the drawer of Andrei's desk and found a journal lying on top. She knew that notebook well. It was the only one Andrei had used for the last ten years. Mechanically, she opened it up and flipped through to the last page: "Louise's brain is a constant source of amazement to me." She put down the journal and began going through his papers. She knew his will was in there somewhere. He himself had shown her the yellow envelope.

The envelope contained two letters, one for Mimi, one for Louise. In his letter to Mimi, Andrei apologized for not leaving any money behind and gave her a list of friends she could turn to for help. He also begged her to reconcile with her family. In his letter to Louise, he called her "my girl" and wrote that she needed to carry on her work for both of them, that she mustn't succumb to feelings of futility, but think of the future. He thanked her for her friendship, the years of life they had shared together, and all the help she had given him. "You're a good sailor, Louise. You could sail a ship out of any storm. Please help Mimi. You're the only she's got. Your A." The letter also contained instructions for the funeral. Andrei asked to be cremated and for them to spread his ashes wherever they saw fit.

In the afternoon they returned to the hospital. Louise had to choose Andrei's clothes for the coffin, since Mimi was still too upset. She took the best she could find: a cambric shirt, a silk tie, a light summer suit, a pair of new shoes. Andrei always had enjoyed dressing nicely.

They still had to decide what to do with the body. The nearest crematorium was in Marseille. The transport and cremation would come to eight thousand francs. Eight thousand!

Louise gasped. She could put the money together, but it seemed like a sin to throw so much money away on something that was ultimately so unimportant. Surely Andrei would have agreed. A burial would come out cheaper, and whether he was burned or rotted away, he wouldn't return from the darkness he had gone into of his own will.

She called a few friends who lived nearby—people she and Andrei had come to know over the years while living in the south of France. An English couple, two Americans. On Tuesday, at ten o'clock in the morning, they buried Andrei at the English cemetery in Nice. The sky shone blue over the tips of the cypress trees, as blue as the sea in the bay below. Louise spoke over the open grave about faith in a free and rational future for humanity, as well as about her personal loss.

15

IN 1931, AFTER ANOTHER UNSUCCESSFUL ATTEMPT at being friends, Louise had written to Mimi Stein:

I would like to take your hand and lead you to a bigger world, more beautiful and more free than any you can imagine. But you refuse. Not because you lack intelligence. But because you cling to the values with which you were raised.

You are wrong, Mimi. I have nothing against your living with Andrei. I have long been accustomed to my lovers leaving me for other women. Often these same women have come to me for advice and I have become their confidante.

What distanced you from me, and from Andrei's friends for good, was your limited, petit bourgeois world, your jealousy of anything you thought might take Andrei away from you.

She wrote the letter after Mimi's last visit to Saint-Tropez, when during dinner someone had whispered in Mimi's ear, "*Ah, vous avez un ménage à trois, alors?*" Mimi had turned red in the face and fled from the table.

Andrei later teased her that it was just a joke. After all, everyone knew he and Louise hadn't slept together in thirty years. That was the last time Mimi went to Saint-Tropez with him. She preferred to stay behind in Saint-Laurent, even if it meant having to contend with the amorous advances of the landlord and fend off the gendarmes who were assigned to keep an eye on the anarchist household and always managed to peek in at just the right moment.

"Alone again?" one of them started in. "If I had a young woman like you, I wouldn't leave her alone at night."

"The gentleman must be quite sure of himself," said the other.

"Or just the opposite." The first one laughed, trying to slip his arm around Mimi's shoulders. "Maybe he's thinking, I'll give my young friend some freedom. What the eyes don't see, the heart won't grieve."

"True, let her enjoy herself with the younger men."

"Communists share everything, don't they?" the first one said, ogling Mimi's breasts.

Mimi spent her nights alone crying, howling like an abandoned dog. But it was still better than going to Saint-Tropez, enduring Louise's comments and watching all those women smile and pout their lips at Andrei, hoping for a kiss.

When Mimi followed Andrei to France, she was twenty-four years old and in love for the first time. She wanted to get married and have a child. Andrei's friends frightened her, especially the women. They talked loudly about sex, drank too much wine, and smoked, and there was a bottomless sadness in their eyes. The only one she liked was Nestor's wife. She had wanted to like Louise at first. She even took her flowers the first time they went to visit.

Louise coldly kissed her on both cheeks. "I don't feel old enough yet for young women to be bringing me flowers," she said. "You can wait till I'm in my grave for that."

Andrei just stood there, pretending not to hear.

On the way home, Mimi cried. The two of them had a quarrel. One of the first, at that time still restrained, of the arguments that were to continue over the course of the next ten years, with their tears, threats, and nighttime walkouts.

Andrei was touched by Mimi's wholehearted devotion. As her first lover, he felt responsible. Louise's freedom wasn't for him. He was afraid of loneliness. But the arguments were draining. He would storm out of the house at night, slamming the door as he shouted he was never coming back. Then he would walk until he reached the coast, where the thundering waves crested and broke against the rocky outcrops. Finally, he could take a breath, calm down, straighten things out in his head. But the emptiness he felt, the overwhelming meaninglessness, was so upsetting, he ended up going straight back home. Anything was better than being alone. Even the stifling darkness. Even the bed soaked with the tears of the human being huddled beside him, a human being who loved him, maybe selfishly and childishly, but who could complain about that? Did anyone have the right to dictate how they should be loved?

AFTER ANDREI'S DEATH, LOUISE LET MIMI move in with her in Saint-Tropez. They lasted two weeks together. As the loss sunk in, Mimi spent most of her time splayed, weeping, on the colorful blanket in Andrei's room, or squatting on the doorstep, staring mutely down at the bay's sparkling surface.

The south coast was deserted. Nancy had left Jack and moved to Venice. She no longer kept in touch with Louise. But when word reached her of Andrei's death, she sent a note of condolence, with a P.S.: "It goes without saying that the house is yours. Do with it as you see fit."

Louise didn't like the thought of giving up the only property she had ever had, but it no longer made sense to stay on the Côte d'Azur. She sold the villa and left for Spain. She was sorry the civil war hadn't broken out sooner, convinced that if Andrei had seen it, he wouldn't have killed himself. He would have overcome the pain and marshaled all his strength, as he had once before, long ago, when the crackdown on anarchists in San Francisco had shaken him out of his lethargy after he got out of prison.

From Spain she went to London, and after that to Canada, where she ended up staying. When the weather was nice, she could see the shores of America on the far side of Lake Ontario. It was almost like being home.

MIMI REFUSED TO GO BACK TO HER PARENTS. She stayed another few months in Saint-Laurent, organizing Andrei's estate. Then she moved to Paris, where she found a position as a secretary with a Viennese marble dealer who had fled Hitler.

But her stomach troubles continued to get worse. The doctor recommended surgery, and she eventually underwent several operations. The last year of her life she spent in a hospital. She died two years after Andrei, at the age of thirty-six.

EPILOGUE

I WAIT BENEATH THE SICKLY TREE the protesters call "sacred." It's stopped raining and the General Assembly at the upper end of the square is going on indefinitely. That direct democracy of theirs works slowly. Somewhere in the crowd are Marius and Mia, and Daniel, too, who came over from England to support his young friends and ended up staying.

The five minutes that Marius promised have long since passed, but I stay where I am. There's nowhere for me to go anyway.

I'm sure they'll ask me about Ilana. She finished her Ph.D. and left New York six months after I did. I saw her once. She came to visit me in Prague from Berlin, where she'd landed a job as a research assistant at the university. Her son and her ex-husband lived in Hamburg. That was the main reason she'd moved to Germany.

We talked mostly about New York and how much we missed it. And also about my book. I still hadn't finished it. I had to earn a living when I returned to Prague, so I went back to teaching and writing for newspapers, which didn't leave me any time to devote to Josef's notebook. We made love once. I didn't hear from her again until a few months later. She invited me to friend her on Facebook, but I declined. It's too frustrating to communicate that way. I couldn't imagine getting any satisfaction out of reading Ilana's mass posts.

Marius still hasn't turned up, but I don't feel like texting him again. I gather up a few more pieces of cardboard that aren't drenched yet and pull my sleeping bag from my backpack. The sky is totally clear now. I've always liked the way the weather changes so fast in New York. Heat or rain, either way, it never lasts more than two days.

It's almost silent except for the distant sound of chanting. Every now and then a siren whoops, a horn honks, then peace and quiet settle back in. Manhattan opens up like a palm extended to the stars.

When I first heard about the encampment, I wasn't optimistic. I didn't believe the young protesters had enough courage and determination to stick it out through the first cold night. But I was wrong. Their numbers increased with each cold night and with every police crackdown. I had to see it for myself!

The police cordon isn't here for nothing. That much is clear. Sooner or later, they'll shut down the camp. Lock up the more hardened protesters, dump the tents on a trash heap. The police are well aware that the movement is lost without a base. It isn't strong enough yet to expand elsewhere without losing its foothold.

Space is key. A place where people can stay, day after day, night after night, sleeping, thinking, eating, creating something. A place that can't be erased with a click of the mouse, that can last as a source of irritation even after it's all over, after the police empty out and seal off the square and its current inhabitants, once again homeless, revert back from being inspiring bearers of change to a ragtag bunch of misfits trying in vain to make people listen.

Even I get annoyed by the nonstop warriors for justice, with their vehement attitudes and furrowed brows. I understand what they want, but I don't see how they plan to achieve it. If I remember correctly, Daniel didn't talk about anything that could be influenced by elections or votes of Congress.

"There is no way to live in accordance with our conscience," Josef had scrawled on the cover of his blue notebook. That was his message to me, the letter he left behind.

The people in the camp here were trying to prove the opposite.

How naïve, I think, this hope for the inner transformation of man. Destined to failure every time.

And yet I feel it, too.

The soggy cardboard digs into my back. How long has it been since I slept under the stars? Ten years, twenty?

Bellevue Literary Press has been publishing prize-winning books since 2007 and is the first and only nonprofit press dedicated to literary fiction and nonfiction at the intersection of the arts and sciences. We believe that science and literature are natural companions for understanding the human experience. Our ultimate goal is to promote science literacy in unaccustomed ways and offer new tools for thinking about our world.

To support our press and its mission, and for our full catalogue of published titles, please visit us at blpress.org.

Bellevue Literary Press
New York